THE FIELD OF ICE

BY

JULES VERNE

THE FIELD OF ICE.

CHAPTER I.

THE DOCTOR'S INVENTORY.

It was a bold project of Hatteras to push his way to the North Pole, and gain for his country the honour and glory of its discovery. But he had done all that lay in human power now, and, after having struggled for nine months against currents and tempests, shattering icebergs and breaking through almost insurmountable barriers, amid the cold of an unprecedented winter, after having outdistanced all his predecessors and accomplished half his task, he suddenly saw all his hopes blasted. The treachery, or rather the despondency, of his worn-out crew, and the criminal folly of one or two leading spirits among them had left him and his little band of men in a terrible situation—helpless in an icy desert, two thousand five hundred miles away from their native land, and without even a ship to shelter them.

However, the courage of Hatteras was still undaunted. The three men which were left him were the best on board his brig, and while they remained he might venture to hope.

After the cheerful, manly words of the captain, the Doctor felt the best thing to be done was to look their prospects fairly in the face, and know the exact state of things. Accordingly, leaving his companions, he stole away alone down to the scene of the explosion.

Of the *Forward*, the brig that had been so carefully built and had become so dear, not a vestige remained. Shapeless blackened fragments, twisted bars of iron, cable ends still smouldering, and here and there in the distance spiral wreaths of smoke, met his eye on all sides. His cabin and all his precious treasures were gone, his books, and instruments, and collections reduced to ashes. As he stood thinking mournfully of his irreparable loss, he was joined by Johnson, who grasped his offered hand in speechless sorrow.

"What's to become of us?" asked the Doctor.

"Who can tell!" was the old sailor's reply.

"Anyhow," said Clawbonny, "do not let us despair! Let us be men!"

"Yes, Mr. Clawbonny, you are right. Now is the time to show our mettle. We are in a bad plight, and how to get out of it, that is the question."

"Poor old brig!" exclaimed the Doctor. "I had grown so attached to her. I loved her as one loves a house where he has spent a life-time."

"Ay! it's strange what a hold those planks and beams get on a fellow's heart."

"And the long-boat—is that burnt?" asked the Doctor.

"No, Mr. Clawbonny. Shandon and his gang have carried it off."

"And the pirogue?"

"Shivered into a thousand pieces? Stop. Do you see those bits of sheet-iron? That is all that remains of it."

"Then we have nothing but the Halkett-boat?"

"Yes, we have that still, thanks to your idea of taking it with you."

"That isn't much," said the Doctor.

"Oh, those base traitors!" exclaimed Johnson. "Heaven punish them as they deserve!"

"Johnson," returned the Doctor, gently, "we must not forget how sorely they have been tried. Only the best remain good in the evil day; few can stand trouble. Let us pity our fellow-sufferers, and not curse them."

For the next few minutes both were silent, and then Johnson asked what had become of the sledge.

"We left it about a mile off," was the reply.

"In charge of Simpson?"

"No, Simpson is dead, poor fellow!"

"Simpson dead!"

"Yes, his strength gave way entirely, and he first sank."

"Poor Simpson! And yet who knows if he isn't rather to be envied?"

"But, for the dead man we have left behind, we have brought back a dying one."

"A dying man?"

"Yes, Captain Altamont."

And in a few words he informed Johnson of their discovery.

"An American!" said Johnson, as the recital was ended.

"Yes, everything goes to prove that. But I wonder what the *Porpoise* was, and what brought her in these seas?"

"She rushed on to her ruin like the rest of foolhardy adventurers; but, tell me, did you find the coal?"

The Doctor shook his head sadly.

"No coal! not a vestige! No, we did not even get as far as the place mentioned by Sir Edward Belcher."

"Then we have no fuel whatever?" said the old sailor.

"No."

"And no provisions?"

"No."

"And no ship to make our way back to England?"

It required courage indeed to face these gloomy realities, but, after a moment's silence, Johnson said again—

"Well, at any rate we know exactly how we stand. The first thing to be done now is to make a hut, for we can't stay long exposed to this temperature."

"Yes, we'll soon manage that with Bell's help," replied the Doctor. "Then we must go and find the sledge, and bring back the American, and have a consultation with Hatteras."

"Poor captain," said Johnson, always forgetting his own troubles, "how he must feel it!"

Clawbonny and Bell found Hatteras standing motionless, his arms folded in his usual fashion. He seemed gazing into space, but his face had recovered its calm, self-possessed expression. His faithful dog stood beside him, like his master, apparently insensible to the biting cold, though the temperature was 32 degrees below zero.

Bell lay on the ice in an almost inanimate condition. Johnson had to take vigorous measures to rouse him, but at last, by dint of shaking and rubbing him with snow, he succeeded.

"Come, Bell," he cried, "don't give way like this. Exert yourself, my man; we must have a talk about our situation, and we need a place to put our heads in. Come and help me, Bell. You haven't forgotten how to make a snow hut, have you? There is an iceberg all ready to hand; we've only got to hollow it out. Let's set to work; we shall find that is the best remedy for us."

Bell tried to shake off his torpor and help his comrade, while Mr. Clawbonny undertook to go and fetch the sledge and the dogs.

"Will you go with him, captain?" asked Johnson.

"No, my friend," said Hatteras, in a gentle tone, "if the Doctor will kindly undertake the task. Before the day ends I must come to some resolution, and I need to be alone to think. Go. Do meantime whatever you think best. I will deal with the future."

Johnson went back to the Doctor, and said—

"It's very strange, but the captain seems quite to have got over his anger. I never heard him speak so gently before."

"So much the better," said Clawbonny. "Believe me, Johnson, that man can save us yet."

And drawing his hood as closely round his head as possible, the Doctor seized his iron-tipped staff, and set out without further delay.

Johnson and Bell commenced operations immediately. They had simply to dig a hole in the heart of a great block of ice; but it was not easy work, owing to the extreme hardness of the material. However, this very hardness guaranteed the solidity of the dwelling, and the further their labours advanced the more they became sheltered.

Hatteras alternately paced up and down, and stood motionless, evidently shrinking from any approach to the scene of explosion.

In about an hour the Doctor returned, bringing with him Altamont lying on the sledge, wrapped up in the folds of the tent. The poor dogs were so exhausted from starvation that they could scarcely draw it along, and they had begun to gnaw their harness. It was, indeed, high time for feasts and men to take food and rest.

While the hut was being still further dug out, the Doctor went foraging about, and had the good fortune to find a little stove, almost undamaged by the explosion. He soon restored it to working trim, and, by the time the hut was completed, had filled it with wood and got it lighted. Before long it was roaring, and diffusing a genial warmth on all sides. The American was brought in and laid on blankets, and the four Englishmen seated themselves round the fire to enjoy their scanty meal of biscuit and hot tea, the last remains of the provisions on the sledge. Not a word was spoken by Hatteras, and the others respected his silence.

When the meal was over, the Doctor rose and went out, making a sign to Johnson to follow.

"Come, Johnson," he said, "we will take an inventory of all we have left. We must know exactly how we are off, and our treasures are scattered in all directions; so we had better begin, and pick them up as fast as possible, for the snow may fall at any moment, and then it would be quite useless to look for anything."

"Don't let us lose a minute, then," replied Johnson. "Fire and food— those are our chief wants."

"Very well, you take one side and I'll take the other, and we'll search from the centre to the circumference."

This task occupied two hours, and all they discovered was a little salt meat, about 50 lbs. of pemmican, three sacks of biscuits, a small stock of chocolate, five or six pints of brandy, and about 2 lbs. of coffee, picked up bean by bean off the ice.

Neither blankets, nor hammocks, nor clothing—all had been consumed in the devouring flame.

This slender store of provisions would hardly last three weeks, and they had wood enough to supply the stove for about the same time.

Now that the inventory was made, the next business was to fetch the sledge. The tired-out dogs were harnessed sorely against their will, and before long returned bringing the few but precious treasures found among the *débris* of the brig. These were safely deposited in the hut, and then Johnson and Clawbonny, half-frozen with their work, resumed their places beside their companions in misfortune.

CHAPTER II.

FIRST WORDS OF ALTAMONT.

About eight o'clock in the evening, the grey snow clouds cleared away for a little, and the stars shone out brilliantly in the sky.

Hatteras seized the opportunity and went out silently to take the altitude of some of the principal constellations. He wished to ascertain if the ice-field was still drifting.

In half an hour he returned and sat down in a corner of the hut, where he remained without stirring all night, motionless as if asleep, but in reality buried in deepest thought.

The next day the snow fell heavily, and the Doctor congratulated himself on his wise forethought, when he saw the white sheet lying three feet thick over the scene of the explosion, completely obliterating all traces of the *Forward*.

It was impossible to venture outside in such weather, but the stove drew capitally, and made the hut quite comfortable, or at any rate it seemed so to the weary, worn out adventurers.

The American was in less pain, and was evidently gradually coming back to life. He opened his eyes, but could not yet speak, for his lips were so affected by the scurvy that articulation was impossible, but he could hear and understand all that was said to him. On learning what had passed, and the circumstances of his discovery, he expressed his thanks by gestures, and the Doctor was too wise to let him know how brief his respite from death would prove. In three weeks at most every vestige of food would be gone.

About noon Hatteras roused himself, and going up to his friends, said—

"We must make up our minds what to do, but I must request Johnson to tell me first all the particulars of the mutiny on the brig, and how this final act of baseness came about."

"What good will that do?" said the Doctor. "The fact is certain, and it is no use thinking over it."

"I differ from your opinion," rejoined Hatteras. "Let me hear the whole affair from Johnson, and then I will banish it from my thoughts."

"Well," said the boatswain, "this was how it happened. I did all in my power to prevent, but——"

"I am sure of that, Johnson; and what's more, I have no doubt the ringleaders had been hatching their plans for some time."

"That's my belief too," said the Doctor.

"And so it is mine," resumed Johnson; "for almost immediately after your departure Shandon, supported by the others, took the command of the ship.

I could not resist him, and from that moment everybody did pretty much as they pleased. Shandon made no attempt to restrain them: it was his policy to make them believe that their privations and toils were at an end. Economy was entirely disregarded. A blazing fire was kept up in the stove, and the men were allowed to eat and drink at discretion; not only tea and coffee was at their disposal, but all the spirits on board, and on men who had been so long deprived of ardent liquors, you may guess the result. They went on in this manner from the 7th to the 15th of January."

"And this was Shandon's doing?" asked Hatteras.

"Yes, captain."

"Never mention his name to me again! Go on, Johnson."

"It was about the 24th or 25th of January, that they resolved to abandon the ship. Their plan was to reach the west coast of Baffin's Bay, and from thence to embark in the boat and follow the track of the whalers, or to get to some of the Greenland settlements on the eastern side. Provisions were abundant, and the sick men were so excited by the hope of return that they were almost well. They began their preparations for departure by making a sledge which they were to draw themselves, as they had no dogs. This was not ready till the 15th of February, and I was always hoping for your arrival, though I half dreaded it too, for you could have done nothing with the men, and they would have massacred you rather than remain on board. I tried my influence on each one separately, remonstrating and reasoning with them, and pointing out the dangers they would encounter, and also the cowardice of leaving you, but it was a mere waste of words; not even the best among them would listen to me. Shandon was impatient to be off, and fixed the 22nd of February for starting. The sledge and the boat were packed as closely as possible with provisions and spirits, and heaps of wood, to obtain which they had hewed the brig down to her water-line. The last day the men ran riot. They completely sacked the ship, and in a drunken paroxysm Pen and two or three others set it on fire. I fought and struggled against them, but they threw me down and assailed me with blows, and then the wretches, headed by Shandon, went off towards the east and were soon out of sight. I found myself alone on the burning ship, and what could I do? The fire- hole was completely blocked up with ice. I had not a single drop of water! For two days the *Forward* struggled with the flames, and you know the rest."

A long silence followed the gloomy recital, broken at length by Hatteras, who said—

"Johnson, I thank you; you did all you could to save my ship, but single-handed you could not resist. Again I thank you, and now let the subject be dropped. Let us unite efforts for our common salvation. There are four of us, four companions, four friends, and all our lives are equally precious. Let each give his opinion on the best course for us to pursue."

"You ask us then, Hatteras," said the Doctor, "we are all devoted to you, and our words come from our hearts. But will you not state you own views first?"

"That would be little use," said Hatteras, sadly; "my opinion might appear interested; let me hear all yours first."

"Captain," said Johnson, "before pronouncing on such an important matter, I wish to ask you a question."

"Ask it, then, Johnson."

"You went out yesterday to ascertain our exact position; well, is the field drifting or stationary?"

"Perfectly stationary. It had not moved since the last reckoning was made. I find we are just where we were before we left, in 80° 15" lat. and 97° 35" long."

"And what distance are we from the nearest sea to the west?"

"About six hundred miles."

"And that sea is——?"

"Smith's Sound," was the reply.

"The same that we could not get through last April?"

"The same."

"Well, captain, now we know our actual situation, we are in a better position to determine our course of action."

"Speak your minds, then," said Hatteras, again burying his head in his hands.

"What do you say, Bell?" asked the Doctor.

"It strikes me the case doesn't need long thinking over," said the carpenter. "We must get back at once without losing a single day or even a single hour, either to the south or west, and make our way to the nearest coast, even if we are two months doing it!"

"We have only food for three weeks," replied Hatteras, without raising his head.

"Very well," said Johnson, "we must make the journey in three weeks, since it is our last chance. Even if we can only crawl on our knees before we get to our destination, we must be there in twenty-five days."

"This part of the Arctic Continent is unexplored. We may have to encounter difficulties. Mountains and glaciers may bar our progress," objected Hatteras.

"I don't see that's any sufficient reason for not attempting it. We shall have to endure sufferings, no doubt, and perhaps many. We shall have to limit ourselves to the barest quantities of food, unless our guns should procure us anything."

"There is only about half a pound of powder left," said Hatteras.

"Come now, Hatteras, I know the full weight of your objections, and I am not deluding myself with vain hopes. But I think I can read your motive. Have you any practical suggestion to offer?"

"No," said Hatteras, after a little hesitation.

"You don't doubt our courage," continued the Doctor. "We would follow you to the last—you know that. But must we not, meantime, give up all hope of reaching the Pole? Your plans have been defeated by treachery. Natural difficulties you might have overcome, but you have been outmatched by perfidy and human weakness. You have done all that man could do, and you would have succeeded I am certain; but situated as we are now, are you not obliged to relinquish your projects for the present, and is not a return to England even positively necessary before you could continue them?"

"Well, captain?" asked Johnson after waiting a considerable time for Hatteras to reply.

Thus interrogated, he raised his head, and said in a constrained tone—

"You think yourselves quite certain then of reaching the Sound, exhausted though you are, and almost without food?"

"No," replied the Doctor, "but there is one thing certain, the Sound won't come to us, we must go to it. We may chance to find some Esquimaux tribes further south."

"Besides, isn't there the chance of falling in with some ship that is wintering here?" asked Johnson.

"Even supposing the Sound is blocked up, couldn't we get across to some Greenland or Danish settlement? At any rate, Hatteras, we can get nothing by remaining here. The route to England is towards the south, not the north."

"Yes," said Bell, "Mr. Clawbonny is right. We must start, and start at once. We have been forgetting our country too long already."

"Is this your advice, Johnson?" asked Hatteras again.

"Yes, captain."

"And yours, Doctor?"

"Yes, Hatteras."

Hatteras remained silent, but his face, in spite of himself, betrayed his inward agitation. The issue of his whole life hung on the decision he had to make, for he felt that to return to England was to lose all! He could not venture on a fourth expedition.

The Doctor finding he did not reply, added—

"I ought also to have said, that there is not a moment to lose. The sledge must be loaded with the provisions at once, and as much wood as possible. I must confess six hundred miles is a long journey, but we can, or rather we must make twenty miles a day, which will bring us to the coast about the 26th of March."

"But cannot we wait a few days yet?" said Hatteras.

"What are you hoping for?" asked Johnson.

"I don't know. Who can tell the future? It is necessary, too, that you should get your strength a little recruited. You might sink down on the road with fatigue, without even a snow hut to shelter you."

"But think of the terrible death that awaits us here," replied the carpenter.

"My friends," said Hatteras, in almost supplicating tones; "you are despairing too soon. I should propose that we should seek our deliverance towards the north, but you would refuse to follow me, and yet why should there not be Esquimaux tribes round about the Pole as well as towards the south? The open sea, of the existence of which we are certified, must wash the shores of continents. Nature is logical in all her doings. Consequently vegetation must be found there when the earth is no longer ice-bound. Is there not a promised land awaiting us in the north from which you would flee?"

Hatteras became animated as he spoke, and Doctor Clawbonny's excitable nature was so wrought upon that his decision began to waver. He was on the point of yielding, when Johnson, with his wiser head and calmer temperament, recalled him to reason and duty by calling out—

"Come, Bell, let us be off to the sledge."

"All right," said Bell, and the two had risen to leave the hut, when Hatteras exclaimed—

"Oh, Johnson! You! you! Well, go! I shall stay, I shall stay!"

"Captain!" said Johnson, stopping in spite of himself.

"I shall stay, I tell you. Go! Leave me like the rest! Come, Duk, you and I will stay together."

The faithful dog barked as if he understood, and settled himself down beside his master. Johnson looked at the Doctor, who seemed at a loss to know what to do, but came to the conclusion at last that the best way, meantime, was to calm Hatteras, even at the sacrifice of a day. He was just about to try the force of his eloquence in this direction, when he felt a light touch on his arm, and turning round saw Altamont who had crawled out of bed and managed to get on his knees. He was trying to speak, but his swollen lips could scarcely make a sound. Hatteras went towards him, and watched his efforts to articulate so attentively that in a few minutes he made out a word that sounded like *Porpoise*, and stooping over him he asked—

"Is it the *Porpoise*?"

Altamont made a sign in the affirmative, and Hatteras went on with his queries, now that he had found a clue.

"In these seas?"

The affirmative gesture was repeated.

"Is she in the north?"

"Yes."

"Do you know her position?"

"Yes."

"Exactly?"

"Yes."

For a minute or so, nothing more was said, and the onlookers waited with palpitating hearts.

Then Hatteras spoke again and said—

"Listen to me. We must know the exact position of your vessel. I will count the degrees aloud, and you; will stop me when I come to the right one."

The American assented by a motion of the head, and Hatteras began—

"We'll take the longitude first. 105°, No? 106°, 107°? It is to the west, I suppose?"

"Yes," replied Altamont.

"Let us go on, then: 109°, 110°, 112°, 114°, 116°, 118°, 120°."

"Yes," interrupted the sick man.

"120° of longitude, and how many minutes? I will count."

Hatteras began at number one, and when he got to fifteen, Altamont made a sign to stop.

"Very good," said Hatteras; "now for the latitude. Are you listening? 80°, 81°, 82°, 83°."

Again the sign to stop was made.

"Now for the minutes: 5', 10', 15', 20', 25', 30', 35'."

Altamont stopped him once more, and smiled feebly.

"You say, then, that the *Porpoise* is in longitude 120° 15', and latitude 83° 35'?"

"Yes," sighed the American, and fell back motionless in the Doctor's arms, completely overpowered by the effort he had made.

"Friends!" exclaimed Hatteras; "you see I was right. Our salvation lies indeed in the north, always in the north. We shall be saved!"

But the joyous, exulting words had hardly escaped his lips before a sudden thought made his countenance change. The serpent of jealousy had stung him, for this stranger was an American, and he had reached three degrees nearer the Pole than the ill-fated *Forward*.

CHAPTER III.

A SEVENTEEN DAYS' MARCH.

These first words of Altamont had completely changed the whole aspect of affairs, but his communication was still incomplete, and, after giving him a little time to rest, the Doctor undertook the task of conversing again with him, putting his questions in such a form that a movement of the head or eyes would be a sufficient answer.

He soon ascertained that the *Porpoise* was a three-mast American ship, from New York, wrecked on the ice, with provisions and combustibles in abundance still on board, and that, though she had been thrown on her side, she had not gone to pieces, and there was every chance of saving her cargo.

Altamont and his crew had left her two months previously, taking the long boat with them on a sledge. They intended to get to Smith's Sound, and reach some whaler that would take them back to America; but one after another succumbed to fatigue and illness, till at last Altamont and two men were all that remained out of thirty; and truly he had survived by a providential miracle, while his two companions already lay beside him in the sleep of death.

Hatteras wished to know why the *Porpoise* had come so far north, and learned in reply that she had been irresistibly driven there by the ice. But his anxious fears were not satisfied with this explanation, and he asked further what was the purpose of his voyage. Altamont said he wanted to make the north-west passage, and this appeared to content the jealous Englishman, for he made no more reference to the subject. "Well," said the Doctor, "it strikes me that, instead of trying to get to Baffin's Bay, our best plan would be to go in search of the *Porpoise*, for here lies a ship a full third of the distance nearer, and, more than that, stocked with everything necessary for winter quarters."

"I see no other course open to us," replied Bell.

"And the sooner we go the better," added Johnson, "for the time we allow ourselves must depend on our provisions."

"You are right, Johnson," returned the Doctor. "If we start to-morrow, we must reach the *Porpoise* by the 15th of March, unless we mean to die of starvation. What do you say, Hatteras?"

"Let us make preparations immediately, but perhaps the route may be longer than we suppose."

"How can that be, captain? The man seems quite sure of the position of his ship," said the Doctor.

"But suppose the ice-field should have drifted like ours?"

Here Altamont, who was listening attentively, made a sign that he wished to speak, and, after much difficulty, he succeeded in telling the Doctor that the *Porpoise* had struck on rocks near the coast, and that it was impossible for her to move.

This was re-assuring information, though it cut off all hope of returning to Europe, unless Bell could construct a smaller ship out of the wreck.

No time was lost in getting ready to start. The sledge was the principal thing, as it needed thorough repair. There was plenty of wood, and, profiting by the experience they had recently had of this mode of transit, several improvements were made by Bell.

Inside, a sort of couch was laid for the American, and covered over with the tent. The small stock of provisions did not add much to the weight, but, to make up the deficiency, as much wood was piled up on it as it could hold.

The Doctor did the packing, and made an exact calculation of how long their stores would last. He found that, by allowing three-quarter rations to each man and full rations to the dogs, they might hold out for three weeks.

Towards seven in the evening, they felt so worn out that they were obliged to give up work for the night; but, before lying down to sleep, they heaped up the wood in the stove, and made a roaring fire, determined to allow themselves this parting luxury. As they gathered round it, basking in the unaccustomed heat, and enjoying their hot coffee and biscuits and pemmican, they became quite cheerful, and forgot all their sufferings.

About seven in the morning they set to work again and by three in the afternoon everything was ready.

It was almost dark, for, though the sun had reappeared above the horizon since the 31st of January, his light was feeble and of short duration. Happily the moon would rise about half-past six, and her soft beams would give sufficient light to show the road.

The parting moment came. Altamont was overjoyed at the idea of starting, though the jolting would necessarily increase his sufferings, for the Doctor would find on board the medicines he required for his cure.

They lifted him on to the sledge, and laid him as comfortably as possible, and then harnessed the dogs, including Duk. One final look towards the icy bed where the *Forward* had been, and the little party set out for the *Porpoise*. Bell was scout, as before; the Doctor and Johnson took each a side of the sledge, and lent a helping hand when necessary; while Hatteras walked behind to keep all in the right track.

They got on pretty quickly, for the weather was good, and the ice smooth and hard, allowing the sledge to glide easily along, yet the temperature was so low that men and dogs were soon panting, and had often to stop and take breath. About seven the moon shone out, and irradiated the whole horizon. Far as the eye could see, there was nothing visible but a wide- stretching level plain of ice, without a solitary hummock or patch to relieve the uniformity.

As the Doctor remarked to his companion, it looked like some vast, monotonous desert.

"Ay! Mr. Clawbonny, it is a desert, but we shan't die of thirst in it at any rate."

"That's a comfort, certainly, but I'll tell you one thing: it proves, Johnson, we must be a great distance from any coast. The nearer the coast, the more numerous the icebergs in general, and you see there is not one in sight."

"The horizon is rather misty, though."

"So it is, but ever since we started, we have been on this same interminable ice-field."

"Do you know, Mr. Clawbonny, that smooth as this ice is, we are going over most dangerous ground? Fathomless abysses lie beneath our feet."

"That's true enough, but they won't engulph us. This white sheet over them is pretty tough, I can tell you. It is always getting thicker too; for in these latitudes, it snows nine days out of ten even in April and May; ay, and in June as well. The ice here, in some parts, cannot be less than between thirty and forty feet thick."

"That sounds reassuring, at all events." said Johnson.

"Yes, we're not like the skaters on the Serpentine—always in danger of falling through. This ice is strong enough to bear the weight of the Custom House in Liverpool, or the Houses of Parliament in Westminster."

"Can they reckon pretty nearly what ice will bear, Mr. Clawbonny?" asked the old sailor, always eager for information.

"What can't be reckoned now-a-days? Yes, ice two inches thick will bear a man; three and a half inches, a man on horse-back; five inches, an eight pounder; eight inches, field artillery; and ten inches, a whole army."

"It is difficult to conceive of such a power of resistance, but you were speaking of the incessant snow just now, and I cannot help wondering where it comes from, for the water all round is frozen, and what makes the clouds?"

"That's a natural enough question, but my notion is that nearly all the snow or rain that we get here comes from the temperate zones. I fancy each of those snowflakes was originally a drop of water in some river, caught up by evaporation into the air, and wafted over here in the shape of clouds; so that it is not impossible that when we quench our thirst with the melted snow, we are actually drinking from the very rivers of our own native land."

Just at this moment the conversation was interrupted by Hatteras, who called out that they were getting out of the straight line. The increasing mist made it difficult to keep together, and at last, about eight o'clock, they determined to come to a halt, as they had gone fifteen miles. The tent was put up and the stove lighted, and after their usual supper they lay down and slept comfortably till morning.

The calm atmosphere was highly favourable, for though the cold became intense, and the mercury was always frozen in the thermometer, they found no difficulty in continuing their route, confirming the truth of Parry's assertion that any man suitably clad may walk abroad with impunity in the lowest temperature, provided there is no wind; while, on the other hand, the least breeze would make the skin smart acutely, and bring on violent headache, which would soon end in death.

On the 5th of March a peculiar phenomenon occurred. The sky was perfectly clear and glittering with stars, when suddenly snow began to fall thick and fast, though there was not a cloud in the heavens and through the white flakes the constellations could be seen shining. This curious display lasted two hours, and ceased before the Doctor could arrive at any satisfactory conclusion as to its cause.

The moon had ended her last quarter, and complete darkness prevailed now for seventeen hours out of the twenty-four. The travellers had to fasten themselves together with a long rope to avoid getting separated, and it was all but impossible to pursue the right course. Moreover, the brave fellows, in spite of their iron will, began to show signs of fatigue. Halts became more frequent, and yet every hour was precious, for the provisions were rapidly coming to an end.

Hatteras hardly knew what to think as day after day went on without apparent result, and he asked himself sometimes whether the *Porpoise* had any actual existence except in Altamont's fevered brain, and more than once the idea even came into his head that perhaps national hatred might have induced the American to drag them along with himself to certain death.

He told the Doctor his suppositions, who rejected them absolutely, and laid them down to the score of the unhappy rivalry that had arisen already between the two captains.

On the 14th of March, after sixteen days' march the little party found themselves only yet in the 82º latitude. Their strength was exhausted, and they had a hundred miles more to go. To increase their sufferings, rations had to be still further reduced. Each man must be content with a fourth part to allow the dogs their full quantity.

Unfortunately they could not rely at all on their guns, for only seven charges of powder were left, and six balls. They had fired at several hares and foxes on the road already, but unsuccessfully.

However, on the 15th, the Doctor was fortunate enough to surprise a seal basking on the ice, and, after several shots, the animal was captured and killed.

Johnson soon had it skinned and cut in pieces, but it was so lean that it was worthless as food, unless its captors would drink the oil like the Esquimaux.

The Doctor was bold enough to make the attempt, but failed in spite of himself.

Next day several icebergs and hummocks were noticed on the horizon. Was this a sign that land was near, or was it some ice-field that had broken up? It was difficult to know what to surmise.

On arriving at the first of these hummocks, the travellers set to work to make a cave in it where they could rest more comfortably than in the tent, and after three hours' persevering toil, were able to light their stove and lie down beside it to stretch their weary limbs.

CHAPTER IV.

THE LAST CHARGE OF POWDER

Johnson was obliged to take the dogs inside the hut, for they would have been soon frozen outside in such dry weather. Had it been snowing they would have been safe enough, for the snow served as a covering, and kept in the natural heat of the animals.

The old sailor, who made a first-rate dog-driver, tried his beasts with the oily flesh of the seal; and found, to his joyful surprise, that they ate it greedily. The Doctor said he was not astonished at this, as in North America the horses were chiefly fed on fish; and he thought that what would satisfy an herbivorous horse might surely content an omnivorous dog.

The whole party were soon buried in deep sleep, for they were fairly overcome with fatigue. Johnson awoke his companions early next morning, and the march was resumed in haste. Their lives depended now on their speed, for provisions would only hold out three days longer.

The sky was magnificent; the atmosphere extremely clear, and the temperature very low. The sun rose in the form of a long ellipse, owing to refraction, which made his horizontal diameter appear twice the length of his vertical.

The Doctor, gun in hand, wandered away from the others, braving the solitude and the cold in the hope of discovering game. He had only sufficient powder left to load three times, and he had just three balls. That was little enough should he encounter a bear, for it often takes ten or twelve shots to have any effect on these enormous animals.

But the brave Doctor would have been satisfied with humbler game. A few hares or foxes would be a welcome addition to their scanty food; but all that day, if even he chanced to see one, either he was too far away, or he was deceived by refraction, and took a wrong aim. He came back to his companions at night with crestfallen looks, having wasted one ball and one charge of powder.

Next day the route appeared more difficult, and the weary men could hardly drag themselves along. The dogs had devoured even the entrails of the seal, and began to gnaw their traces.

A few foxes passed in the distance, and the Doctor lost another ball in attempting to shoot them.

They were forced to come to a halt early in the evening, though the road was illumined by a splendid Aurora Borealis; for they could not put one foot before the other.

Their last meal, on the Sunday evening, was a very sad one—if no providential help came, their doom was sealed.

Johnson set a few traps before going to sleep, though he had no baits to put inside them. He was very disappointed to find them all empty in the morning, and was returning gloomily to the hut, when he perceived a bear of huge dimensions. The old sailor took it into his head that Heaven had sent this beast specially for him to kill; and without waking his comrades, he seized the Doctor's gun, and was soon in pursuit of his prey. On reaching the right distance, he took aim; but, just as his finger touched the trigger, he felt his arm tremble. His thick gloves hampered him, and, flinging them hastily off, he took up the gun with a firmer grasp. But what a cry of agony escaped him! The skin of his fingers stuck to the gun as if it had been

red-hot, and he was forced to let it drop. The sudden fall made it go off, and the last ball was discharged in the air.

The Doctor ran out at the noise of the report, and understood all at a glance. He saw the animal walking quietly off, and poor Johnson forgetting his sufferings in his despair.

"I am a regular milksop!" he exclaimed, "a cry-baby, that can't stand the least pain! And at my age, too!"

"Come, Johnson; go in at once, or you will be frost-bitten. Look at your hands—they are white already! Come, come this minute."

"I am not worth troubling about, Mr. Clawbonny," said the old boatswain. "Never mind me!"

"But you must come in, you obstinate fellow. Come, now, I tell you; it will be too late presently."

At last he succeeded in dragging the poor fellow into the tent, where he made him plunge his hands into a

bowl of water, which the heat of the stove kept in a liquid state, though still cold. Johnson's hands had hardy touched it before it froze immediately.

"You see it was high time you came in; I should have been forced to amputate soon," said the Doctor.

Thanks to his endeavours, all danger was over in about an hour, but he was advised to keep his hands at a good distance from the stove for some time still.

That morning they had no breakfast. Pemmican and salt beef were both done. Not a crumb of biscuit remained. They were obliged to content themselves with half a cup of hot coffee, and start off again.

They scarcely went three miles before they were compelled to give up for the day. They had no supper but coffee, and the dogs were so ravenous that they were almost devouring each other.

Johnson fancied he could see the bear following them in the distance, but he made no remark to his companions. Sleep forsook the unfortunate men, and their eyes grew wild and haggard.

Tuesday morning came, and it was thirty-four hours since they had tasted a morsel of food. Yet these brave, stout-hearted men continued their march, sustained by their superhuman energy of purpose. They pushed the sledge themselves, for the dogs could no longer draw it.

At the end of two hours, they sank exhausted. Hatteras urged them to make a fresh attempt, but his entreaties and supplications were powerless; they could not do impossibilities.

"Well, at any rate," he said, "I won't die of cold if I must of hunger." He set to work to hew out

a hut in an iceberg, aided by Johnson, and really they looked like men digging their own tomb.

It was hard labour, but at length the task was accomplished. The little house was ready, and the miserable men took up their abode in it.

In the evening, while the others lay motionless, a sort of hallucination came over Johnson, and he began raving about bears.

The Doctor roused himself from his torpor, and asked the old man what he meant, and what bear he was talking about.

"The bear that is following us," replied Johnson.

"A bear following us?"

"Yes, for the last two days!"

"For the last two days! You have seen him?"

"Yes, about a mile to leeward."

"And you never told me, Johnson!"

"What was the good!"

"True enough," said the Doctor; "we have not a single bail to send after him!"

"No, not even a bit of iron!"

The Doctor was silent for a minute, as if thinking. Then he said—

"Are you quite certain the animal is following us?"

"Yes, Mr. Clawbonny, he is reckoning on a good feed of human flesh!"

"Johnson!" exclaimed the Doctor, grieved at the despairing mood of his companion.

"He is sure enough of his meal!" continued the

"You have no ball!"

"I'll make one."

"You have no lead!"

"No, but I have mercury."

So saying, he took the thermometer, which stood at 50° above zero, and went outside and laid it on a block of ice. Then he came in again, and said, "Tomorrow! Go to sleep, and wait till the sun rises."

With the first streak of dawn next day, the Doctor and Johnson rushed out to look at the thermometer. All the mercury had frozen into a compact cylindrical mass. The Doctor broke the tube and took it out. Here was a hard piece of metal ready for use.

"It is wonderful, Mr. Clawbonny; you ought to be a proud man."

"Not at all, my friend, I am only gifted with a good memory, and I have read a great deal."

"How did that help you?"

"Why, I just happened to recollect a fact related by Captain Ross in his voyages. He states that they pierced a plank, an inch thick, with a bullet made of mercury. Oil would even have suited my purpose, for, he adds, that a ball of frozen almond oil splits through a post without breaking in pieces."

"It is quite incredible!"

"But it is a fact, Johnson. Well, come now, this bit of metal may save our lives. We'll leave it exposed to the air a little while, and go and have a look for the bear."

Just then Hatteras made his appearance, and the

Doctor told him his project, and showed him the mercury.

The captain grasped his hand silently, and the three hunters went off in quest of their game.

The weather was very clear, and Hatteras, who was a little ahead of the others, speedily discovered the bear about three hundred yards distant, sitting on his hind quarters sniffing the air, evidently scenting the intruders on his domains.

"There he is!" he exclaimed.

"Hush!" cried the Doctor.

But the enormous quadruped, even when he perceived his antagonists, never stirred, and displayed neither fear nor anger. It would not be easy to get near him, however, and Hatteras said—

"Friends, this is no idle sport, our very existence is at stake; we must act prudently."

"Yes," replied the Doctor, "for we have but the one shot to depend upon. We must not miss, for if Away they went, while the old boatswain slipped behind a hummock, which completely hid him from the bear, who continued still in the same place and in the same position.

CHAPTER V.

THE SEAL AND THE BEAR.

"You know, Doctor," said Hatteras, as they returned to the hut, "the polar bears subsist almost entirely on seals. They'll lie in wait for them beside the crevasses for whole days, ready to strangle them the moment their heads appear above the surface. It is not likely, then, that a bear will be frightened of a seal."

"I think I see what you are after, but it is dangerous."

"Yes, but there is more chance of success than in trying any other plan, so I mean to risk it. I am going to dress myself in the seal's skin, and creep along the ice. Come, don't let us lose time. Load the gun and give it me."

The Doctor could not say anything, for he would have done the same himself, so he followed Hatteras silently to the sledge, taking with him a couple of hatchets for his own and Johnson's use.

Hatteras soon made his *toilette*, and slipped into the skin, which was big enough to cover him almost entirely.

"Now, then, give me the gun," he said, "and you be off to Johnson. I must try and steal a march on my adversary."

"Courage, Hatteras!" said the Doctor, handing him the weapon, which he had carefully loaded meanwhile.

"Never fear! but be sure you don't show yourselves till I fire."

The Doctor soon joined the old boatswain behind the hummock, and told him what they had been doing. The bear was still there, but moving restlessly about, as if he felt the approach of danger.

In a quarter of an hour or so the seal made his appearance on the ice. He had gone a good way round, so as to come on the bear by surprise, and every movement was so perfect an imitation of a seal, that even the Doctor would have been deceived if he had not known it was Hatteras.

"It is capital!" said Johnson, in a low voice. The bear had instantly caught sight of the supposed seal, for he gathered himself up, preparing to make a spring as the animal came nearer, apparently seeking to return to his native element, and unaware of the enemy's proximity. Bruin went to work with extreme prudence, though his eyes glared with greedy desire to clutch the coveted prey, for he had probably been fasting a month, if not two. He allowed his victim to get within ten paces of him, and then sprang forward with a tremendous bound, but stopped short, stupefied and frightened, within three steps of Hatteras, who started up that moment, and, throwing off his disguise, knelt on one knee, and aimed straight at the bear's heart. He fired, and the huge monster rolled back on the ice.

"Forward! Forward!" shouted the Doctor, hurrying towards Hatteras, for the bear had reared on his hind legs, and was striking the air with one paw and tearing up the snow to stanch his wound with the other.

Hatteras never moved, but waited, knife in hand. He had aimed well, and fired with a sure and steady aim. Before either of his companions came up he had plunged the knife in the animal's throat, and made an end of him, for he fell down at once to rise no more.

"Hurrah! Bravo!" shouted Johnson and the Doctor, but Hatteras was as cool and unexcited as possible, and stood with folded arms gazing at his prostrate foe.

"It is my turn now," said Johnson. "It is a good thing the bear is killed, but if we leave him out here much longer, he will get as hard as a stone, and we shall be able to do nothing with him."

He began forthwith to strip the skin off, and a fine business it was, for the enormous quadruped was almost as large as an ox. It measured nearly nine feet long, and four round, and the great tusks in his jaws were three inches long.

On cutting the carcase open, Johnson found nothing but water in the stomach. The beast had evidently had no food for a long time, yet it was very fat, and weighed fifteen hundred pounds. The hunters were so famished that they had hardly patience to carry home the flesh to be cooked, and it needed all the Doctor's persuasion to prevent them eating it raw.

On entering the hut, each man with a load on his back, Clawbonny was struck with the coldness that pervaded the atmosphere. On going up to the stove he found the fire black out. The exciting business of the morning had made Johnson neglect his accustomed duty of replenishing the stove.

The Doctor tried to blow the embers into a flame, but finding he could not even get a red spark, he went out to the sledge to fetch tinder, and get the steel from Johnson.

The old sailor put his hand into his pocket, but was surprised to find the steel missing. He felt in the other pockets, but it was not there. Then he went into the hut again, and shook the blanket he had slept in all night, but his search was still unsuccessful.

He went back to his companions and said—

"Are you sure, Doctor, you haven't the steel?"

"Quite, Johnson."

"And you haven't it either, captain?"

"Not I!" replied Hatteras.

"It has always been in your keeping," said the Doctor.

"Well, I have not got it now!" exclaimed Johnson, turning pale.

"Not got the steel!" repeated the Doctor, shuddering involuntarily at the bare idea of its loss, for it was all the means they had of procuring a fire.

"Look again, Johnson," he said.

The boatswain hurried to the only remaining place he could think of, the hummock where he had stood to watch the bear. But the missing treasure was nowhere to be found, and the old sailor returned in despair.

Hatteras looked at him, but no word of reproach escaped his lips. He only said—

"This is a serious business, Doctor."

"It is, indeed!" said Clawbonny.

"We have not even an instrument, some glass that we might take the lens out of, and use like a burning glass."

"No, and it is a great pity, for the sun's rays are quite strong enough just now to light our tinder."

"Well," said Hatteras, "we must just appease our hunger with the raw meat, and set off again as soon as we can, to try to discover the ship."

"Yes!" replied Clawbonny, speaking to himself, absorbed in his own reflections. "Yes, that might do at a pinch! Why not? We might try."

"What are you dreaming about?" asked Hatteras.

"An idea has just occurred to me."

"An idea come into your head, Doctor," exclaimed Johnson; "then we are saved!"

"Will it succeed? that's the question."

"What's your project?" said Hatteras.

"We want a lens; well, let us make one."

"How?" asked Johnson.

"With a piece of ice."

"What? Do you think that would do?"

"Why not? All that is needed is to collect the sun's rays into one common focus, and ice will serve that purpose as well as the finest crystal."

"Is it possible?" said Johnson.

"Yes, only I should like fresh water ice, it is harder and more transparent than the other."

"There it is to your hand, if I am not much mistaken," said Johnson, pointing to a hummock close by.

"I fancy that is fresh water, from the dark look of it, and the green tinge."

"You are right. Bring your hatchet, Johnson."

A good-sized piece was soon cut off, about a foot in diameter, and the Doctor set to work. He began by chopping it into rough shape with the hatchet; then he operated upon it more carefully with his knife, making as smooth a surface as possible, and finished the polishing process with his fingers, rubbing away until he had obtained as transparent a lens as if it had been made of magnificent crystal.

The sun was shining brilliantly enough for the Doctor's experiment. The tinder was fetched, and held beneath the lens so as to catch the rays in full power. In a few seconds it took fire, to Johnson's rapturous delight.

He danced about like an idiot, almost beside himself with joy, and shouted, "Hurrah! hurrah!" while Clawbonny hurried back into the hut and rekindled the fire. The stove was soon roaring, and it was not many minutes before the savoury odour of broiled bear-steaks roused Bell from his torpor.

What a feast this meal was to the poor starving men may be imagined. The Doctor, however, counselled moderation in eating, and set the example himself.

"This is a glad day for us," he said, "and we have no fear of wanting food all the rest of our journey. Still we must not forget we have further to go yet, and I think the sooner we start the better."

"We cannot be far off now," said Altamont, who could almost articulate perfectly again; "we must be within forty-eight hours' march of the *Porpoise*."

"I hope we'll find something there to make a fire with," said the Doctor, smiling. "My lens does well enough at present; but it needs the sun, and there are plenty of days when he does not make his appearance here, within less than four degrees of the pole."

"Less than four degrees!" repeated Altamont, with a sigh; "yes, my ship went further than any other has ever ventured."

"It is time we started," said Hatteras, abruptly.

"Yes," replied the Doctor, glancing uneasily at the two captains.

The dogs were speedily harnessed to the sledge, and the march resumed.

As they went along, the Doctor tried to get out of Altamont the real motive that had brought him so far north. But the American made only evasive replies, and Clawbonny whispered in old Johnson's ear—

"Two men we've got that need looking after."

"You are right," said Johnson.

"Hatteras never says a word to this American, and I must say the man has not shown himself very grateful. I am here, fortunately."

"Mr. Clawbonny," said Johnson, "now this Yankee has come back to life again, I must confess I don't much like the expression of his face."

"I am much mistaken if he does not suspect the projects of Hatteras."

"Do you think his own were similar?"

"Who knows? These Americans, Johnson, are bold, daring fellows. It is likely enough an American would try to do as much as an Englishman."

"Then you think that Altamont—"

"I think nothing about it, but his ship is certainly on the road to the North Pole."

"But didn't Altamont say that he had been caught among the ice, and dragged there irresistibly?"

"He said so, but I fancied there was a peculiar smile on his lips while he spoke."

"Hang it! It would be a bad job, Mr. Clawbonny, if any feeling of rivalry came between two men of their stamp."

"Heaven forfend! for it might involve the most serious consequences, Johnson."

"I hope Altamont will remember he owes his life to us?"

"But do we not owe ours to him now? I grant, without us, he would not be alive at this moment, but without him and his ship, what would become of us?"

"Well, Mr. Clawbonny, you are here to keep things straight anyhow, and that is a blessing."

"I hope I may manage it, Johnson."

The journey proceeded without any fresh incident, but on the Saturday morning the travellers found themselves in a region of quite an altered character. Instead of the wide smooth plain of ice that had hitherto stretched before them, overturned icebergs and broken hummocks covered the horizon; while the frequent blocks of fresh-water ice showed that some coast was near.

Next day, after a hearty breakfast off the bear's paws, the little party continued their route; but the road became toilsome and fatiguing. Altamont lay watching the horizon with feverish anxiety—an anxiety shared by all his companions, for, according to the last reckoning made by Hatteras, they were now exactly in latitude 83° 35" and longitude 120° 15", and the question of life or death would be decided before the day was over.

At last, about two o'clock in the afternoon, Altamont started up with a shout that arrested the whole party, and pointing to a white mass that no eye but his could have distinguished from the surrounding icebergs, exclaimed in a loud, ringing voice, "The *Porpoise*."

CHAPTER VI.

THE *PORPOISE*

It was the 24th of March, and Palm Sunday, a bright, joyous day in many a town and village of the Old World, but in this desolate region what mournful silence prevailed! No willow branches here with their silvery blossom — not even a single withered leaf to be seen — not a blade of grass!

Yet this was a glad day to the travellers, for it promised them speedy deliverance from the death that had seemed so inevitable.

They hastened onward, the dogs put forth renewed energy, and Duk barked his loudest, till, before long, they arrived at the ship. The *Porpoise* was completely buried under the snow. All her masts and rigging had been destroyed in the shipwreck, and she was lying on a bed of rocks so entirely on her side that her hull was uppermost.

They had to knock away fifteen feet of ice before they could even catch a glimpse of her, and it was not without great difficulty that they managed to get on board, and made the welcome discovery that the provision stores had not been visited by any four-footed marauders. It was quite evident, however, that the ship was not habitable.

"Never mind!" said Hatteras, "we must build a snow-house, and make ourselves comfortable on land."

"Yes, but we need not hurry over it," said the Doctor; "let us do it well while we're about it, and for a time we can make shift on board; for we must build a good, substantial house, that will protect us from the bears as well as the cold. I'll undertake to be the architect, and you shall see what a first-rate job I'll make of it."

"I don't doubt your talents, Mr. Clawbonny," replied Johnson; "but, meantime, let us see about taking up our abode here, and making an inventory of the stores we find. There does not seem a boat visible of any description, and I fear these timbers are in too bad a condition to build a new ship out of them."

"I don't know that," returned Clawbonny, "time and thought do wonders; but our first business is to build a house, and not a ship; one thing at a time, I propose."

"And quite right too," said Hatteras; "so we'll go ashore again."

They returned to the sledge, to communicate the result of their investigation to Bell and Altamont; and about four in the afternoon the five men installed themselves as well as they could on the wreck. Bell had managed to make a tolerably level floor with planks and spars; the stiffened cushions and hammocks were placed round the stove to thaw, and were soon fit for use. Altamont, with the Doctor's assistance, got on board without much trouble, and a sigh of satisfaction escaped him as if he felt himself once more at home—a sigh which to Johnson's ear boded no good.

The rest of the day was given to repose, and they wound up with a good supper off the remains of the bear, backed by a plentiful supply of biscuit and hot tea.

It was late next morning before Hatteras and his companions woke, for their minds were not burdened now with any solicitudes about the morrow, and they might sleep as long as they pleased. The poor fellows felt like colonists safely arrived at their destination, who had forgotten all the sufferings of the voyage, and thought only of the new life that lay before them.

"Well, it is something at all events," said the Doctor, rousing himself and stretching his arms, "for a fellow not to need to ask where he is going to find his next bed and breakfast."

"Let us see what there is on board before we say much," said Johnson.

The *Porpoise* has been thoroughly equipped and provisioned for a long voyage, and, on making an inventory of what stores remained, they found 6150 lbs. of flour, fat, and raisins; 2000 lbs. of salt beef and pork, 1500 lbs. of pemmican; 700 lbs. of sugar, and the same of chocolate; a chest and a half of tea, weighing 96 lbs.; 500 lbs. of rice; several barrels of preserved fruits and vegetables; a quantity of lime-juice, with all sorts of medicines, and 300 gallons of rum and brandy. There was also a large supply of gunpowder, ball, and shot, and coal and wood in abundance.

Altogether, there was enough to last those five men for more than two years, and all fear of death from starvation or cold was at an end.

"Well, Hatteras, we're sure of enough to live on now," said the Doctor, "and there is nothing to hinder us reaching the Pole."

"The Pole!" echoed Hatteras.

"Yes, why not? Can't we push our way overland in the summer months?"

"We might overland; but how could we cross water?"

"Perhaps we may be able to build a boat out of some of the ship's planks."

"Out of an American ship!" exclaimed the captain, contemptuously.

Clawbonny was prudent enough to make no reply, and presently changed the conversation by saying—

"Well, now we have seen what we have to depend upon, we must begin our house and store-rooms. We have materials enough at hand; and, Bell, I hope you are going to distinguish yourself," he added.

"I am ready, Mr. Clawbonny," replied Bell; "and, as for material, there is enough for a town here with houses and streets."

"We don't require that; we'll content ourselves with imitating the Hudson's Bay Company. They entrench themselves in fortresses against the Indians and wild beasts. That's all we need—a house one side and stores the other, with a wall and two bastions. I must try to make a plan."

"Ah! Doctor, if you undertake it," said Johnson, "I am sure you'll make a good thing of it."

"Well, the first part of the business is to go and choose the ground. Will you come with us Hatteras?"

"I'll trust all that to you, Doctor," replied the captain. "I'm going to look along the coast."

Altamont was too feeble yet to take part in any work, so he remained on the ship, while the others commenced to explore the unknown continent.

On examining the coast, they found that the *Porpoise* was in a sort of bay bristling with dangerous rocks, and that to the west, far as the eye could reach, the sea extended, entirely frozen now, though if Belcher and Penny were to be believed, open during the summer months. Towards the north, a promontory stretched out into the sea, and about three miles away was an island of moderate size. The roadstead thus formed would have afforded safe anchorage to ships, but for the difficulty of entering it. A considerable distance inland there was a solitary mountain, about 3000 feet high, by the Doctor's reckoning; and half-way up the steep rocky cliffs that rose from the shore, they noticed a circular plateau, open on three sides to the bay and sheltered on the fourth by a precipitous wall, 120 feet high.

This seemed to the Doctor the very place for this house, from its naturally fortified situation. By cutting steps in the ice, they managed to climb up and examine it more closely.

They were soon convinced they could not have a better foundation, and resolved to commence operations forthwith, by removing the hard snow more than ten feet deep, which covered the ground, as both dwelling and storehouses must have a solid foundation.

This preparatory work occupied the whole of Monday, Tuesday, and Wednesday. At last they came to hard granite close in grain, and containing garnets and felspar crystals, which flew out with every stroke of the pickaxe.

The dimensions and plan of the snow-house were then settled by the Doctor. It was to be divided into three rooms, as all they needed was a bed-room, sitting-room and kitchen. The sitting-room was to be in the middle, the kitchen to the left, and the bed-room to the right.

For five days they toiled unremittingly. There was plenty of material, and the walls required to be thick enough to resist summer thaws. Already the house began to present an imposing appearance. There were four windows in front, made of splendid sheets of ice, in Esquimaux fashion, through which the light came softly in as if through frosted glass.

Outside there was a long covered passage between the two windows of the sitting-room. This was the entrance hall, and it was shut in by a strong door taken from the cabin of the *Porpoise*. The Doctor was highly delighted with his performance when all was finished, for though it would have been difficult to say to what style of architecture it belonged, it was strong, and that was the chief thing.

The next business was to move in all the furniture of the *Porpoise*. The beds were brought first and laid down round the large stove in the sleeping room; then came chairs, tables, arm-chairs, cupboards, and benches for the sitting-room, and finally the ship furnaces and cooking utensils for the kitchen. Sails spread on the ground did duty for carpets, and also served for inner doors.

The walls of the house were over five feet thick, and the windows resembled port-holes for cannon. Every part was as solid as possible, and what more was wanted? Yet if the Doctor could have had his way, he would have made all manner of ornamental additions, in humble imitation of the Ice Palace built in St. Petersburgh in January, 1740, of which he had read an account. He amused his companions after work in the evening by describing its grandeur, the cannons in front, and statues of exquisite beauty, and the wonderful elephant that spouted water out of his trunk by day and flaming naphtha by night—all cut out of ice. He also depicted the interior, with tables, and toilette tables, mirrors, candelabra, tapers, beds, mattresses, pillows, curtains, time-pieces, chairs, playing-cards, wardrobes, completely fitted up—in fact, everything in the way of furniture that could be mentioned, and the whole entirely composed of ice.

It was on Easter Sunday, the 31st of March, when the travellers installed themselves in their new abode and after holding divine service in the sitting-room, they devoted the remainder of the day to rest.

Next morning they set about building the storehouses and powder magazine. This took a whole week longer, including the time spent in unloading the vessel, which was a task of considerable difficulty, as the temperature was so low, that they could not work for many hours at a time. At length on the 8th of April, provisions, fuel, and ammunition were all safe on *terra firma,* and deposited in their respective places. A sort of kennel was constructed a little distance from the house for the Greenland dogs, which the Doctor dignified by the name of "Dog Palace." Duk shared his master's quarters.

All that now remained to be done was to put a parapet right round the plateau by way of fortification.

By the 15th this was also completed, and the snow-house might bid defiance to a whole tribe of Esquimaux, or any other hostile invaders, if indeed any human beings whatever were to be found on this unknown continent, for Hatteras, who had minutely examined the bay and the surrounding coast, had not been able to discover the least vestiges of the huts that are generally met with on shores frequented by Greenland tribes. The shipwrecked sailors of the *Porpoise* and *Forward* seemed to be the first whose feet had ever trod this lone region.

CHAPTER VII.

AN IMPORTANT DISCUSSION.

While all these preparations for winter were going on Altamont was fast regaining strength. His vigorous constitution triumphed, and he was even able to lend a helping hand in the unlading of the ship. He was a true type of the American, a shrewd, intelligent man, full of energy and resolution, enterprising, bold, and ready for anything. He was a native of New York, he informed his companions, and had been a sailor from his boyhood.

The *Porpoise* had been equipped and sent out by a company of wealthy merchants belonging to the States, at the head of which was the famous Grinnell.

There were many points of resemblance between Altamont and Hatteras, but no affinities. Indeed, any similarity that there was between them, tended rather to create discord than to make the men friends. With a greater show of frankness, he was in reality far more deep and crafty than Hatteras. He was more free and easy, but not so true-hearted, and somehow his apparent openness did not inspire such confidence as the Englishman's gloomy reserve.

The Doctor was in constant dread of a collision between the rival captains, and yet one must command inevitably, and which should it be! Hatteras had the men, but Altamont had the ship, and it was hard to say whose was the better right.

It required all the Doctor's tact to keep things smooth, for the simplest conversation threatened to lead to strife.

At last, in spite of all his endeavours, an outbreak occurred on the occasion of a grand banquet by way of "house-warming," when the new habitation was completed.

This banquet was Dr Clawbonny's idea. He was head-cook, and distinguished himself by the concoction of a wonderful pudding, which would positively have done no dishonour to the *cuisine* of the Lord Chancellor of England.

Bell most opportunely chanced to shoot a white hare and several ptarmigans, which made an agreeable variety from the pemmican and salt meat.

Clawbonny was master of the ceremonies, and brought in his pudding, adorning himself with the insignia of his office—a big apron, and a knife dangling at his belt.

As Altamont did not conform to the teetotal *régime* of his English companions, gin and brandy were set on the table after dinner, and the others, by the Doctor's orders, joined him in a glass for once, that the festive occasion might be duly honoured. When the different toasts were being drunk, one was given to the United States, to which Hatteras made no response.

This important business over, the Doctor introduced an interesting subject of conversation by saying—

"My friends, it is not enough to have come thus far in spite of so many difficulties; we have something more yet to do. I propose we should bestow a name on this continent, where we have found friendly shelter and rest, and not only on the continent, but on the several bays, peaks, and promontories that we meet with. This has been invariably done by navigators and is a most necessary proceeding."

"Quite right," said Johnson, "when once a place is named, it takes away the feeling of being castaways on an unknown shore."

"Yes," added Bell, "and we might be going on some expedition and obliged to separate, or go out hunting, and it would make it much easier to find one another if each locality had a definite name."

"Very well; then," said the Doctor, "since we are all agreed, let us go steadily to work."

Hatteras had taken no part in the conversation as yet, but seeing all eyes fixed on him, he rose at last, and said—

"If no one objects, I think the most suitable name we can give our house is that of its skilful architect, the best man among us. Let us call it 'Doctor's House.' "

"Just the thing!" said Bell.

"First rate!" exclaimed Johnson, " 'Doctor's House!' "

"We cannot do better," chimed in Altamont. "Hurrah for Doctor Clawbonny."

Three hearty cheers were given, in which Duk joined lustily, barking his loudest.

"It is agreed then," said Hatteras, "that this house is to be called 'Doctor's House.' "

The Doctor, almost overcome by his feelings, modestly protested against the honour; but he was obliged to yield to the wishes of his friends, and the new habitation was formally named "Doctor's House."

"Now, then," said the Doctor, "let us go onto name the most important of our discoveries."

"There is that immense sea which surrounds us, unfurrowed as yet by a single ship."

"A single ship!" repeated Altamont. "I think you have forgotten the *Porpoise*, and yet she certainly did not get here overland,"

"Well, it would not be difficult to believe she had," replied Hatteras, "to see on what she lies at present."

"True, enough, Hatteras," said Altamont, in a piqued tone; "but, after all, is not that better than being blown to atoms like the *Forward*?"

Hatteras was about to make some sharp retort, but Clawbonny interposed.

"It is not a question of ships, my friends," he said, "but of a fresh sea."

"It is no new sea," returned Altamont; "it is in every Polar chart, and has a name already. It is called the Arctic Ocean, and I think it would be very inconvenient to alter its designation. Should we find out by and by, that, instead of being an ocean it is only a strait or gulf, it will be time enough to alter it then."

"So be it," said Hatteras.

"Very well, that is an understood thing, then," said the Doctor, almost regretting that he had started a discussion so pregnant with national rivalries.

"Let us proceed with the continent where we find ourselves at present," resumed Hatteras. "I am not aware that any name whatever has been affixed to it, even in the most recent charts."

He looked at Altamont as he spoke, who met his gaze steadily, and said—

"Possibly you may be mistaken again, Hatteras."

"Mistaken! What! This unknown continent, this virgin soil——"

"Has already a name," replied Altamont, coolly.

Hatteras was silent, but his lip quivered.

"And what name has it, then?" asked the Doctor, rather astonished at Altamont's affirmation.

"My dear Clawbonny," replied the American, "it is the custom, not to say the right, of every navigator to christen the soil on which he is the first to set foot. It appears to me, therefore, that it is my privilege and duty on this occasion to exercise my prerogative, and—"

"But, sir," interrupted Johnson, rather nettled at his *sang froid*.

"It would be a difficult matter to prove that the *Porpoise* did not come here, even supposing she reached this coast by land," continued Altamont, without noticing Johnson's protest. "The fact is indisputable," he added looking at Hatteras.

"I dispute the claim," said the Englishman, restraining himself by a powerful effort. "To name a country, you must first discover it, I suppose, and that you certainly did not do. Besides, but for us, where would you have been, sir, at this moment, pray? Lying twenty feet deep under the snow."

"And without me, sir," retorted Altamont, hotly, "without me and my ship, where would you all be at this moment? Dead, from cold and hunger."

"Come, come, friends," said the Doctor, "don't get to words, all that can be easily settled. Listen to me."

"Mr. Hatteras," said Altamont, "is welcome to name whatever territories he may discover, should he succeed in discovering any; but this continent belongs to me. I should not even consent to its having two names like Grinnell's Land, which is also called Prince Albert's Land, because it was discovered almost simultaneously by an Englishman and an American. This is quite another matter; my right of priority is incontestable. No ship before mine ever touched this shore, no foot before mine ever trod this soil. I have given it a name, and that name it shall keep."

"And what is that name?" inquired the Doctor.

"New America," replied Altamont.

Hatteras trembled with suppressed passion, but by a violent effort restrained himself.

"Can you prove to me," said Altamont, "that an Englishman has set foot here before an American?"

Johnson and Bell said nothing, though quite as much offended as the captain by Altamont's imperious tone. They felt that reply was impossible.

For a few minutes there was an awkward silence, which the Doctor broke by saying—

"My friends, the highest human law is justice. It includes all others. Let us be just, then, and don't let any bad feeling get in among us. The priority of Altamont seems to me indisputable. We will take our revenge by and by, and England will get her full share in our future discoveries. Let the name New America stand for the continent itself, but I suppose Altamont has not yet disposed of all the bays, and capes, and headlands it contains, and I imagine there will be nothing to prevent us calling this bay Victoria Bay?"

"Nothing whatever, provided that yonder cape is called Cape Washington," replied Altamont.

"You might choose a name, sir," exclaimed Hatteras, almost beside himself with passion, "that is less offensive to an Englishman."

"But not one which sounds so sweet to an American," retorted Altamont, proudly.

"Come, come," said the Doctor, "no discussion on that subject. An American has a perfect right to be proud of his great countryman! Let us honour genius wherever it is met with; and since Altamont has made his choice, let us take our turn next; let the captain——"

"Doctor!" interrupted Hatteras, "I have no wish that my name should figure anywhere on this continent, seeing that it belongs to America."

"Is this your unalterable determination?" asked Clawbonny.

"It is."

The Doctor did not insist further.

"Very well, we'll have it to ourselves then," he continued, turning to Johnson and Bell. "We'll leave our traces behind us. I propose that the island we see out there, about three miles away from the shore, should be called Isle Johnson, in honour of our boatswain,"

"Oh, Mr. Clawbonny," began Johnson, in no little confusion.

"And that mountain that we discovered in the west we will call Bell Mount, if our carpenter is willing."

"It is doing me too much honour," replied Bell.

"It is simple justice," returned the Doctor.

"Nothing could be better," said Altamont.

"Now then, all we have to do is to christen our fort," said the Doctor, "about that there will be no discussion, I hope, for it is neither to our gracious sovereign Queen Victoria, nor to Washington, that we owe our safety and shelter here, but to God, who brought about our meeting, and by so doing saved us all. Let our little fort be called Fort Providence."

"Your remarks are just," said Altamont; "no name could be more suitable."

"Fort Providence," added Johnson, "sounds well too. In our future excursions, then, we shall go by Cape Washington to Victoria Bay, and from thence to Fort Providence, where we shall find food and rest at Doctor's House!"

"The business is settled then so far," resumed the Doctor. "As our discoveries multiply we shall have other names to give; but I trust, friends, we shall have no disputes about them, for placed as we are, we need all the help and love we can give each other. Let us be strong by being united. Who knows what dangers yet we may have to brave, and what sufferings to endure before we see our native land once more. Let us be one in heart though five in number, and let us lay aside all feelings of rivalry. Such feelings are bad enough at all times, but among us they would be doubly wrong. You understand me, Altamont, and you, Hatteras?"

Neither of the captains replied, but the Doctor took no notice of their silence, and went on to speak of other things. Sundry expeditions were planned to forage for fresh food. It would soon be spring, and hares and partridges, foxes and bears would reappear. So it was determined that part of every day should be spent in hunting and exploring this unknown continent of New America.

CHAPTER VIII.

AN EXCURSION TO THE NORTH OF VICTORIA BAY

Next morning Clawbonny was out by dawn of day. Clambering up the steep, rocky wall, against which the Doctor's House leaned, he succeeded, though with considerable difficulty, in reaching the top, which he found terminated abruptly in a sort of truncated cone. From this elevation there was an extensive view over a vast tract of country, which was all disordered and convulsed as if it had undergone some volcanic commotion. Sea and land, as far as it was possible to distinguish one from the other, were covered with a sheet of ice.

A new project struck the Doctor's mind, which was soon matured and ripe for execution. He lost no time in going back to the snow house, and consulting over it with his companions.

"I have got an idea," he said; "I think of constructing a lighthouse on the top of that cone above our heads."

"A lighthouse!" they all exclaimed.

"Yes, a lighthouse. It would be a double advantage. It would be a beacon to guide us in distant excursions, and also serve to illumine our *plateau* in the long dreary winter months."

"There is no doubt," replied Altamont, "of its utility; but how would you contrive to make it?"

"With one of the lanterns out of the *Porpoise*."

"All right; but how will you feed your lamp? With seal oil?"

"No, seal oil would not give nearly sufficient light. It would scarcely be visible through the fog."

"Are you going to try to make gas out of our coal then?"

"No, not that either, for gas would not be strong enough; and, worse still, it would waste our combustibles."

"Well," replied Altamont; "I'm at a loss to see how you—"

"Oh, I'm prepared for everything after the mercury bullet, and the ice lens, and Fort Providence. I believe Mr. Clawbonny can do anything," exclaimed Johnson.

"Come, Clawbonny, tell us what your light is to be, then," said Altamont.

"That's soon told," replied Clawbonny. "I mean to have an electric light."

"An electric light?"

"Yes, why not? Haven't you a galvanic battery on board your ship?"

"Yes."

"Well, there will be no difficulty then in producing an electric light, and that will cost nothing, and be far brighter."

"First-rate?" said Johnson; "let us set to work at once."

"By all means. There is plenty of material. In an hour we can raise a pillar of ice ten feet high, and that is quite enough.

Away went the Doctor, followed by his companions, and the column was soon erected and crowned with a ship lantern. The conducting wires were properly adjusted within it, and the pile with which they communicated fixed up in the sitting-room, where the warmth of the stove would protect it from the action of the frost.

As soon as it grew dark the experiment was made, and proved a complete success. An intense brilliant light streamed from the lantern and illumined the entire plateau and the plains beneath.

Johnson could not help clapping his hands, half beside himself with delight.

"Well, I declare, Mr. Clawbonny," he exclaimed, "you're our sun now."

"One must be a little of everything, you know," was Clawbonny's modest reply.

It was too cold. however, even to stand admiring more than a minute, and the whole party were glad enough to get indoors again, and tuck themselves up in their warm blankets.

A regular course of life commenced now, though uncertain weather and frequent changes of temperature made it sometimes impracticable to venture outside the hut at all, and it was not till the Saturday after the installation, that a day came that was favourable enough for a hunting excursion; when Bell, and Altamont, and the Doctor determined to take advantage of it, and try to replenish their stock of provisions.

They started very early in the morning, each armed with a double- barrelled gun and plenty of powder and shot, a hatchet, and a snow knife.

The weather was cloudy, but Clawbonny put the galvanic battery in action before he left, and the bright rays of the electric light did duty for the glorious orb of day, and in truth was no bad substitute, for the light was equal to three thousand candles, or three hundred gas burners.

It was intensely cold, but dry, and there was little or no wind. The hunters set off in the direction of Cape Washington, and the hard snow so favoured their march, that in three hours they had gone fifteen miles, Duk jumping and barking beside them all the way. They kept as close to the coast as possible, but found no trace of human habitation and indeed scarcely a sign of animal life. A few snow birds, however, darting to and fro announced the approach of spring and the return of the animal creation. The sea was still entirely frozen over, but it was evident from the open breathing holes in the ice, that the seals had been quite recently on the surface. In one part the holes were so numerous, that the Doctor said to his companions that he had no doubt that when summer came, they would be seen there in hundreds, and would be easily captured, for on unfrequented shores they were not so difficult of approach. But once frighten them and they all vanish as if by enchantment, and never return to the spot again. "Inexperienced hunters," he said, "have often lost a whole shoal by attacking them, *en masse*, with noisy shouts instead of singly and silently."

"Is it for the oil or skin that they are mostly hunted?"

"Europeans hunt them for the skin, but the Esquimaux eat them. They live on seals, and nothing is so delicious to them as a piece of the flesh, dipped in the blood and oil.

After all, cooking has a good deal to do with it, and I'll bet you something I could dress you cutlets you would not turn up your nose at, unless for their black appearance."

"We'll set you to work on it," said Bell, "and I'll eat as much as you like to please you."

"My good Bell, you mean to say to please yourself, but your voracity would never equal the Green-landers', for they devour from ten to fifteen pounds of meat a day."

"Fifteen pounds!" said Bell. "What stomachs!"

"Arctic stomachs," replied the Doctor, "are prodigious; they can expand at will, and, I may add, contract at will; so that they can endure starvation quite as well as abundance. When an Esquimaux sits down to dinner he is quite thin, and by the time he has finished, he is so corpulent you would hardly recognize him. But then we must remember that one meal sometimes has to last a whole day."

"This voracity must be peculiar to the inhabitants of cold countries," said Altamont.

"I think it is," replied the Doctor. "In the Arctic regions people must eat enormously: it is not only one of the conditions of strength, but of existence. The Hudson's Bay Company always reckoned on this account 8 lbs. of meat to each man a day, or 12 lbs. of fish, or 2 lbs. of pemmican."

"Invigorating regimen, certainly!" said Bell.

"Not so much as you imagine, my friend. An Indian who guzzles like that can't do a whit better day's work than an Englishman, who has his pound of beef and pint of beer."

"Things are best as they are, then, Mr. Clawbonny."

"No doubt of it; and yet an Esquimaux meal may well astonish us. In Sir John Ross's narrative, he states his surprise at the appetites of his guides. He tells us that two of them—just two mind—devoured a quarter of a buffalo in one morning. They cut the meat in long narrow strips, and the mode of eating was either for the one to bite off as much as his mouth could hold, and then pass it on to the other, or to leave the long ribbons of meat dangling from the mouth and devour them gradually like boa-constrictors, lying at full length on the ground."

"Faugh!" exclaimed Bell, "what disgusting brutes!"

"Every man has his own fashion of dining," remarked the philosophical American.

"Happily," said the Doctor.

"Well, if eating is such an imperative necessity in these latitudes, it quite accounts for all the journals of Arctic travellers being so full of eating and drinking."

"You are right," returned the Doctor. "I have been struck by the same fact; but I think it arises not only from the necessity of full diet, but from the extreme difficulty sometimes in procuring it. The thought of food is always uppermost in the mind, and naturally finds mention in the narrative."

"And yet," said Altamont, "if my memory serves me right, in the coldest parts of Norway the peasants do not seem to need such substantial fare. Milk diet is their staple food, with eggs, and bread made of the bark of the birch-tree; a little salmon occasionally, but never meat; and still they are fine hardy fellows."

"It is an affair of organization out of my power to explain," replied Clawbonny; "but I have no doubt that if these same Norwegians were transplanted to Greenland, they would learn to eat like the Esquimaux by the second or third generation. Even if we ourselves were to remain in this blessed country long, we should be as bad as the Esquimaux, even if we escaped becoming regular gluttons."

"I declare, Mr. Clawbonny, you make me feel hungry with talking so much about eating," exclaimed Bell.

"Not I!" said Altamont. "It rather sickens me, and makes me loathe the sight of a seal. But, stop, I do believe we are going to have the chance of a dinner off one, for I am much mistaken if that's not something alive lying on those lumps of ice yonder!"

"It is a walrus!" exclaimed the Doctor. "Be quiet, and let us get up to him."

Clawbonny was right, it was a walrus of huge dimensions, disporting himself not more than two hundred yards away. The hunters separated, going in different directions, so as to surround the animal and cut off all retreat. They crept along cautiously behind the hummocks, and managed to get within a few paces of him unperceived, when they fired simultaneously.

The walrus rolled over, but speedily got up again, and tried to make his escape, but Altamont fell upon him with his hatchet, and cut off his dorsal fins. He made a desperate resistance, but was overpowered by his enemies, and soon lay dead, reddening the ice-field with his blood.

It was a fine animal, measuring more than fifteen feet in length, and would have been worth a good deal for the oil; but the hunters contented themselves with cutting off the most savoury parts, and left the rest to the ravens, which had just begun to make their appearance.

Night was drawing on, and it was time to think of returning to Fort Providence. The moon had not yet risen, but the sky was serene and cloudless, and already glittering with stars—magnificent stars.

"Come," said the Doctor, "let us be off, for it is getting late. Our hunting has not been very successful; but still, if a man has found something for his supper, he need not grumble. Let us go the shortest road, however, and get quickly home without losing our way. The stars will guide us."

They resolved to try a more direct route back by going further inland, and avoiding the windings of the coast; but, after some hours' walking, they found themselves no nearer Doctor's House, and it was evident that they must have lost their way. The question was raised whether to construct a hut and rest till morning, or proceed; but Clawbonny insisted on going on, as Hatteras and Johnson would be so uneasy.

"Duk will guide us," he said; "he won't go wrong. His instinct can dispense with star and compass. Just let us keep close behind him."

They did well to trust to Duk, for very speedily a faint light appeared in the horizon almost like a star glimmering through the mist, which hung low above the ground.

"There's our lighthouse!" exclaimed the Doctor.

"Do you think it is, Mr. Clawbonny?" said Bell.

"I'm certain of it! Come on faster." The light became stronger the nearer they approached, and soon they were walking in a bright luminous track, leaving their long shadows behind them on the spotless snow.

Quickening their steps, they hastened forward, and in another half hour they were climbing the ascent to Fort Providence.

CHAPTER IX.

COLD AND HEAT.

Hatteras and Johnson had been getting somewhat uneasy at the prolonged absence of their companions, and were delighted to see them back safe and sound. The hunters were no less glad to find themselves once more in a warm shelter, for the temperature had fallen considerably as night drew on, and the thermometer outside was 73° below zero.

The poor hunters were half frozen, and so worn out that they could hardly drag their limbs along; but the stoves were roaring and crackling cheerily, and the big kitchen fire waiting to cook such game as might be brought in. Clawbonny donned his official apron again, and soon had his seal cutlets dressed and smoking on the table. By nine o'clock the whole party were enjoying a good supper, and Bell couldn't help exclaiming—

"Well, even at the risk of being taken for an Esquimaux, I must confess eating is the most important business if one has to winter in these regions. A good meal isn't to be sneezed at."

They all had their mouths crammed too full to speak, but the Doctor signified his agreement with Bell's views by an approving nod.

The cutlets were pronounced first-rate, and it seemed as if they were, for they were all eaten, to the very last morsel.

For dessert they had coffee, which the Doctor brewed himself in a French coffee-pot over spirits-of-wine. He never allowed anybody but himself to concoct this precious beverage; for he made a point of serving it boiling hot, always declaring it was not fit to drink unless it burnt his tongue. This evening he took it so scalding that Altamont exclaimed—

"You'll skin your throat!"

"Not a bit of it," was the Doctor's reply.

"Then your palate must be copper-sheathed," said Johnson.

"Not at all, friends. I advise you to copy my example. Many persons, and I am one, can drink coffee at a temperature of 131°."

"131°?" said Altamont; "why, that is hotter than the hand could bear!"

"Of course it is, Altamont, for the hand could not bear more than 122°, but the palate and tongue are less sensitive."

"You surprise me."

"Well, I will convince you it is fact," returned Clawbonny, and taking up a thermometer, he plunged it into the steaming coffee. He waited till the mercury rose as high as 131° and then withdrew it, and swallowed the liquid with evident gusto.

Bell tried to follow his example, but burnt his mouth severely.

"You are not used to it," said the Doctor, coolly.

"Can you tell us, Clawbonny," asked Altamont, "what is the highest temperature that the human body can bear."

"Yes, several curious experiments have been made in that respect. I remember reading of some servant girls, in the town of Rochefoucauld, in France, who could stay ten minutes in a baker's large oven when the temperature was 300°, while potatoes and meat were cooking all round them."

"What girls!" exclaimed Altamont.

"Well, there is another case, where eight of our own countrymen— Fordyce, Banks, Solander, Blagdin, Home, Nooth, Lord Seaforth, and Captain Phillips—went into one as hot as 200°, where eggs and beef were frizzling."

"And they were Englishmen!" said Bell, with a touch of national pride.

"Oh, the Americans could have done better than that," said Altamont.

"They would have roasted," returned the Doctor, laughing. " At all events they have never tried it, so I shall stand up for my countrymen. There is one more instance I recollect, and really it is so incredible, that it would be impossible to believe it, if it were not attested by unimpeachable evidence. The Duke of Ragusa and

Dr. Jung, a Frenchman and an Austrian, saw a Turk plunge into a bath at 170°."

"But that is not so astonishing as those servant girls, or our own countrymen," said Johnson.

"I beg your pardon," replied Clawbonny; "there is a great difference between plunging into hot air and hot water. Hot air produces perspiration, which protects the skin, but boiling water scalds. The *maximum* heat of baths is 107°, so that this Turk must have been an extraordinary fellow to endure such temperature."

"What is the mean temperature, Mr. Clawbonny, of animated beings?" asked Johnson.

"That varies with the species," replied the Doctor. "Birds have the highest, especially the duck and the hen. The mammalia come next, and human beings. The temperature of Englishmen averages 101°."

"I am sure Mr. Altamont is going to claim a higher rate for his countrymen," said Johnson, smiling.

"Well, sure enough, we've some precious hot ones among us, but as I never have put a thermometer down their throats to ascertain, I can't give you statistics."

"There is no sensible difference," said the Doctor, "between men of different races when they are placed under the same conditions, whatever their food may be. I may almost say their temperature would be the same at the Equator as the Pole."

"Then the heat of our bodies is the same here as in England," replied Altamont.

"Just about it. The other species of mammalia are generally hotter than human beings. The horse, the hare, the elephant, the porpoise, and the tiger are nearly the same; but the cat, the squirrel, the rat, the panther, the sheep, the ox, the dog, the monkey, and the goat, are as high as 103°; and the pig is 104°."

"Rather humiliating to us," put in Altamont.

"Then come the amphibia and the fish," resumed the Doctor, " whose temperature varies with that of the water. The serpent has a temperature of 86°, the frog 70°, and the shark several degrees less. Insects appear to have the temperature of air and water."

"All this is very well," interrupted Hatteras, who had hitherto taken no part in the conversation, "and we are obliged to the Doctor for his scientific information; but we are really talking as if we were going to brave the heat of the torrid zone. I think it would be far more seasonable to speak of cold, if the Doctor could tell us what is the lowest temperature on record."

"I can enlighten you on that too," replied the Doctor. "There are a great number of memorable winters, which appear to have come at intervals of about forty-one years. In 1364, the Rhone was frozen over as far as Arles; in 1408, the Danube was frozen throughout its entire extent, and the wolves crossed the Cattigut on firm ground; in 1509, the Adriatic and the Mediterranean were frozen at Venice and Marseilles, and the Baltic on the 10th of April; in 1608, all the cattle died in England from the cold; in 1789, the Thames was frozen as far as Gravesend; and the frightful winter of 1813 will long be remembered in France. The earliest and longest ever known in the present century was in 1829. So much for Europe."

"But here, within the Polar circle, what is the lowest degree?" asked Altamont.

"My word!" said the Doctor. "I think we have experienced the lowest ourselves, for one day the thermometer was 72° below zero, and, if my memory serves me right, the lowest temperature mentioned hitherto by Arctic voyagers has been 61° at Melville Island, 65° at Port Felix, and 70° at Fort Reliance."

"Yes," said Hatteras, "it was the unusual severity of the winter that barred our progress, for it came on just at the worst time possible."

"You were stopped, you say?" asked Altamont, looking fixedly at the captain.

"Yes, in our voyage west," the Doctor hastened to reply.

"Then the maximum and minimum temperatures," said Altamont, resuming the conversation, "are about 200° apart. So you see, my friends, we may make ourselves easy."

"But if the sun were suddenly extinguished," suggested Johnson, "would not the earth's temperature be far lower?"

"There is no fear of such a catastrophe; but, even should it happen, the temperature would be scarcely any different."

"That's curious."

"It is; but Fourrier, a learned Frenchman, has proved the fact incontestably. If it were not the case, the difference between day and night would be far greater, as also the degree of cold at the Poles. But now I think, friends, we should be the better of a few hours' sleep. Who has charge of the stove?"

"It is my turn to-night," said Bell.

"Well, pray keep up a good fire, for it is a perishing night."

"Trust me for that," said Bell. "But do look out, the sky is all in a blaze."

"Ay! it is a magnificent aurora," replied the Doctor, going up to the window. "How beautiful! I never tire gazing at it."

No more he ever did, though his companions had become so used to such displays that they hardly noticed them now. He soon followed the example of the others, however, and lay down on his bed beside the fire, leaving Bell to mount guard.

CHAPTER X.

WINTER PLEASURES

It is a dreary affair to live at the Pole, for there is no going out for many long months, and nothing to break the weary monotony.

The day after the hunting excursion was dark and snowy, and Clawbonny could find no occupation except polishing up the ice walls of the hut as they became damp with the heat inside, and emptying out the snow which drifted into the long passage leading to the inner door. The "Snow- House" stood out well, defying storm and tempest, and the snow only seemed to increase the thickness of the walls.

The storehouses, too, did not give way the least; but though they were only a few yards off, it was found necessary to lay in enough provisions for the day, as very often the weather made it almost impossible to venture that short distance.

The unloading of the *Porpoise* turned out to have been a wise precaution, for she was slowly but surely being crashed to pieces by the silent, irresistible pressure around her. Still the Doctor was always hoping enough planks might be sufficiently sound to construct a small vessel to convey them back to England, but the right time to build had not come.

The five men were consequently compelled to spend the greater part of the day in complete idleness. Hatteras lolled on his bed absorbed in thought. Altamont smoked or dozed, and the Doctor took care not to disturb either of them, for he was in perpetual fear of a quarrel between them.

At meal times he always led the conversation away from irritating topics and sought, as far as possible, to instruct and interest all parties. Whenever he was not engaged with the preparation of his notes, he gave them dissertations on history, geography, or meteorology, handling his subject in an easy, though philosophical manner, drawing lessons from the most trivial incidents. His inexhaustible memory was never at a loss for fact or illustration when his good humour and geniality made him the life and soul of the little company. He was implicitly trusted by all, even by Hatteras, who cherished a deep affection for him.

Yet no man felt the compulsory confinement more painfully than Clawbonny. He longed ardently for the breaking up of the frost to resume his excursions though he dreaded the rivalry that might ensue between the two captains.

Yet things must come to a crisis soon or late, and meantime he resolved to use his best endeavors to bring both parties to a better mind, but to reconcile an American and an Englishman was no easy task. He and Johnson had many a talk on the subject, for the old sailor's views quite coincided with his own as to the difficult complications which awaited them in the future.

However, the bad weather continued, and leaving Fort Providence, even for an hour, was out of the question. Day and night they were pent up in these glittering ice-walls, and time hung heavily on their hands, at least on all but the Doctor's, and he always managed to find some occupation for himself.

"I declare," said Altamont, one evening; "life like this is not worth having. We might as well be some of those reptiles that sleep all the winter. But I suppose there is no help for it."

"I am afraid not," said the Doctor; "unfortunately we are too few in number to get up any amusement."

"Then you think if there were more of us, we should find more to do?"

"Of course: when whole ships' crews have wintered here, they have managed to while away the time famously."

"Well, I must say I should like to know how. It would need a vast amount of ingenuity to extract anything amusing out of our circumstances. I suppose they did not play at charades?"

"No, but they introduced the press and the theatre."

"What? They had a newspaper?" exclaimed the American.

"They acted a comedy?" said Bell.

"That they did," said the Doctor. "When Parry wintered at Melville Island, he started both amusements among his men, and they met with great success."

"Well, I must confess, I should like to have been there," returned Johnson; "for it must have been rather curious work."

"Curious and amusing too, my good Johnson. Lieutenant Beechey was the theatre manager, and Captain Sabina chief editor of the newspaper called 'The Winter Chronicle, or the Gazette of Northern Georgia.' "

"Good titles," said Altamont.

"The newspaper appeared daily from the 1st of November, 1819, to the 20th of March, 1820. It reported the different excursions, and hunting parties, and accidents, and adventures, and published amusing stories. No doubt the articles were not up to the 'Spectator' or the 'Daily Telegraph,' but the readers were neither critical nor *blasé*, and found great pleasure in their perusal."

"My word!" said Altamont. "I should like to read some of the articles."

"Would you? Well, you shall judge for yourself."

"What! can you repeat them from memory?"

"No; but you had Parry's Voyages on board the *Porpoise*, and I can read you his own narrative if you like."

This proposition was so eagerly welcomed that the Doctor fetched the book forthwith, and soon found the passage in question.

"Here is a letter," he said, "addressed to the editor."

" 'Your proposition to establish a journal has been received by us with the greatest satisfaction. I am convinced that, under your direction, it will be a great source of amusement, and go a long way to lighten our hundred days of darkness.

" 'The interest I take in the matter myself has led me to study the effect of your announcement on my comrades, and I can testify, to use reporter's language, that the thing has produced an immense sensation.

" 'The day after your prospectus appeared, there was an unusual and unprecedented demand for ink among us, and our green tablecloth was deluged with snippings and parings of quill-pens, to the injury of one of our servants, who got a piece driven right under his nail. I know for a fact that Sergeant Martin had no less than nine pen-knives to sharpen.

" 'It was quite a novel sight to see all the writing-desks brought out, which had not made their appearance for a couple of months, and judging by the reams of paper visible, more than one visit must have been made to the depths of the hold.

" 'I must not forget to tell you, that I believe attempts will be made to slip into your box sundry articles which are not altogether original, as they have been published already. I can declare that, no later than last night, I saw an author bending over his desk, holding a volume of the "Spectator" open with one hand, and thawing the frozen ink in his pen at the lamp with the other. I need not warn you to be on your guard against such tricks, for it would never do for us to have articles in our "Winter Chronicle" which our great-grandfathers read over their breakfast-tables a century ago.' "

"Well, well," said Altamont, "there is a good deal of clever humour in that writer. He must have been a sharp fellow."

"You're right. Here is an amusing catalogue of Arctic tribulations:—

" 'To go out in the morning for a walk, and the moment you put your foot outside the ship, find yourself immersed in the cook's water-hole.

" 'To go out hunting, and fall in with a splendid reindeer, take aim, and find your gun has gone off with a flash in the pan, owing to damp powder.

" 'To set out on a march with a good supply of soft new bread in your pocket, and discover, when you want to eat, that it has frozen so hard that you would break your teeth if you attempted to bite it through.

" 'To rush from the table when it is reported that a wolf is in sight, and on coming back to find the cat has eaten your dinner.

" 'To be returning quietly home from a walk, absorbed in profitable meditation, and suddenly find yourself in the embrace of a bear.'

"We might supplement this list ourselves," said the Doctor, "to almost any amount, for there is a sort of pleasure in enumerating troubles when one has got the better of them."

"I declare," said Altamont, "this 'Winter Journal' is an amusing affair. I wish we could subscribe to it."

"Suppose we start one," said Johnson.

"For us five!" exclaimed Clawbonny; "we might do for editors, but there would not be readers enough."

"No, nor spectators enough, if we tried to get up a comedy," added Altamont.

"Tell us some more about Captain Parry's theatre," said Johnson; "did they play new pieces?"

"Certainly. At first two volumes on board the 'Hecla' were gone through, but as there was a performance once a fortnight, this *repertoire* was soon exhausted. Then they had to improvise fresh plays; Parry himself composed one which had immense success. It was called 'The North-West Passage, or the End of the Voyage.' "

"A famous title," said Altamont; "but I must confess, if I had chosen such a subject, I should have been at a loss for the *dénouement*."

"You are right," said Bell; "who can say what the end will be?"

"What does that matter?" replied Mr. Clawbonny. "Why should we trouble about the last act, while the first ones are going on well. Leave all that to Providence, friends; let us each play our own *rôle* as perfectly as we can, and since the *dénouement* belongs to the Great Author of all things, we will trust his skill. He will manage our affairs for us, never fear."

"Well, we'd better go and dream about it," said Johnson, "for it's getting late, and it is time we went to bed," said Johnson.

"You're in a great hurry, old fellow," replied the Doctor.

"Why would you sit up, Mr. Clawbonny? I am so comfortable in my bed, and then I always have such good dreams. I dream invariably of hot countries, so that I might almost say, half my life is spent in the tropics, and half at the North Pole."

"You're a happy man, Johnson," said Altamont, "to be blessed with such a fortunate organization."

"Indeed I am," replied Johnson.

"Well, come, after that it would be positive cruelty to keep our good friend pining here," said the Doctor, "his tropical sun awaits him, so let's all go to bed."

CHAPTER XI

TRACES OF BEARS

On the 26th of April during the night there was a sudden change in the weather. The thermometer fell several degrees, and the inmates of Doctor's House could hardly keep themselves warm even in their beds. Altamont had charge of the stove, and he found it needed careful replenishing to preserve the temperature at 50° above zero.

This increase of cold betokened the cessation of the stormy weather, and the Doctor hailed it gladly as the harbinger of his favourite hunting and exploring expeditions.

He rose early next morning, and climbed up to the top of the cone. The wind had shifted north, the air was clear, and the snow firm and smooth to the tread.

Before long the five companions had left Doctor's House, and were busily engaged in clearing the heavy masses of snow off the roof and sides, for the house was no longer distinguishable from the plateau, as the snow had drifted to a depth of full fifteen feet. It took two hours to remove the frozen snow, and restore the architectural form of the dwelling. At length the granite foundations appeared, and the storehouses and powder magazines were once more accessible.

But as, in so uncertain a climate, a storm might cut off their supplies any day, they wisely resolved to provide for any such emergency by carrying over a good stock of provisions to the kitchen; and then Clawbonny, Altamont, and Bell started off with their guns in search of game, for the want of fresh food began to be urgently felt.

The three companions went across the east side of the cone, right down into the centre of the far-stretching, snow-covered plain beneath, but they did not need to go far, for numerous traces of animals appeared on all sides within a circle of two miles round Fort Providence.

After gazing attentively at these traces for some minutes, the hunters looked at each other silently, and then the Doctor exclaimed:—

"Well, these are plain enough, I think!"

"Ay, only too plain," added Bell, "bears have been here!"

"First rate game!" said Altamont. "There's only one fault about it."

"And what is that?" asked Bell.

"What do you mean?"

"I mean this—there are distinct traces of five bears, and five bears are rather too much for five men."

"Are you sure there are five?" said Clawbonny.

"Look and see for yourself. Here is one footprint, and there is another quite different. These claws are far wider apart than those; and see here, again, that paw belongs to a much smaller bear. I tell you, if you look carefully, you will see the marks of all five different bears distinctly."

"You're right," said Bell, after a close inspection.

"If that's the case, then," said the Doctor, "we must take care what we're about, and not be foolhardy, for these animals are starving after the severe winter, and they might be extremely dangerous to encounter and, since we are sure of their number——"

"And of their intentions, too," put in Altamont.

"You think they have discovered our presence here?"

"No doubt of it, unless we have got into a bear-pass, but then, why should these footprints be in a circle round our fort? Look, these animals have come from the south-east, and stopped at this place, and commenced to reconnoitre the coast."

"You're right," said the Doctor, "and, what's more, it is certain that they have been here last night."

"And other nights before that," replied Altamont.

"I don't think so," rejoined Clawbonny. "It is more likely that they waited till the cessation of the tempest, and were on their way down to the bay, intending to catch seals, when they scented us."

"Well, we can easily find out if they come tonight," said Altamont.

"How?"

"By effacing all the marks in a given place, and if to-morrow, we find fresh ones, it will be evident that Fort Providence is the goal for which the bears are bound."

"Very good, at any rate we shall know, then, what we have to expect."

The three hunters set to work, and scraped the snow over till all the footprints were obliterated for a considerable distance.

"It is singular, though," said Bell, "that bears could scent us all that way off; we have not been burning anything fat which might have attracted them."

"Oh!" replied the Doctor, "bears are endowed with a wonderfully keen sense of smell, and a piercing sight; and, more than that, they are extremely intelligent, almost more so than any other animal. They have smelt something unusual; and, besides, who can tell whether they have not even found their way as far as our plateau during the tempest?"

"But then, why did they stop here last night?" asked Altamont.

"Well, that's a question I can't answer, but there is no doubt they will continue narrowing their circles, till they reach Fort Providence."

"We shall soon see," said Altamont.

"And, meantime, we had best go on," added the Doctor, "and keep a sharp look out."

But not a sign of anything living was visible, and after a time they returned to the snow-house.

Hatteras and Johnson were informed how matters stood, and it was resolved to maintain a vigilant watch. Night came, but nothing disturbed its calm splendour—nothing was heard to indicate approaching danger.

Next morning at early dawn, Hatteras and his companions, well armed, went out to reconnoitre the state of the snow. They found the same identical footmarks, but somewhat nearer. Evidently the enemy was bent on the siege of Fort Providence.

"But where can the bears be?" said Bell.

"Behind the icebergs watching us," replied the Doctor. "Don't let us expose ourselves imprudently."

"What about going hunting, then?" asked Altamont.

"We must put it off for a day or two, I think, and rub out the marks again, and see if they are renewed to-morrow."

The Doctor's advice was followed, and they entrenched themselves for the present in the fort. The lighthouse was taken down, as it was not of actual use meantime, and might help to attract the bears. Each took it in turn to keep watch on the upper plateau.

The day passed without a sign of the enemy's existence, and next morning, when they hurried eagerly out to examine the snow, judge their astonishment to find it wholly untouched!

"Capital!" exclaimed Altamont. "The bears are put off the scent; they have no perseverance, and have grown tired waiting for us. They are off, and a good riddance. Now let us start for a day's hunting."

"Softly, softly," said the Doctor; "I'm not so sure they have gone. I think we had better wait one day more. It is evident the bears have not been here last night, at least on this side; but still—"

"Well, let us go right round the plateau, and see how things stand," said the impatient Altamont.

"All right," said Clawbonny. "Come along."

Away they went, but it was impossible to scrutinize carefully a track of two miles, and no trace of the enemy was discoverable.

"Now, then, can't we go hunting?" said Altamont.

"Wait till to-morrow," urged the Doctor again.

His friend was very unwilling to delay, but yielded the point at last, and returned to the fort.

As on the preceding night, each man took his hour's watch on the upper plateau. When it came to Altamont's turn, and he had gone out to relieve Bell, Hatteras called his old companions round him. The Doctor left his desk and Johnson his cooking, and hastened to their captain's side, supposing he wanted to talk over their perilous situation; but Hatteras never gave it a thought.

"My friends," he said, "let us take advantage of the American's absence to speak of business. There are things which cannot concern him, and with which I do not choose him to meddle."

Johnson and Clawbonny looked at each other, wondering what the captain was driving at.

"I wish," he continued, "to talk with you about our plans for the future."

"All right! talk away while we are alone," said the Doctor.

"In a month, or six weeks at the outside, the time for making distant excursions will come again. Have you thought of what we had better undertake in summer?"

"Have you, captain?" asked Johnson.

"Have I? I may say that not an hour of my life passes without revolving in my mind my one cherished purpose. I suppose not a man among you intends to retrace his steps?"

No one replied, and Hatteras went on to say—

"For my own part, even if I must go alone, I will push on to the North Pole. Never were men so near it before, for we are not more than 360 miles distant at most, and I will not lose such an opportunity without making every attempt to reach it, even though it be an impossibility. What are your views, Doctor?"

"Your own, Hatteras."

"And yours, Johnson?"

"Like the Doctor's."

"And yours, Bell?"

"Captain," replied the carpenter, "it is true we have neither wives nor children waiting us in England, but, after all, it is one's country— one's native land! Have you no thoughts of returning home?"

"We can return after we have discovered the Pole quite as well as before, and even better. Our difficulties will not increase, for as we near the Pole we get away from the point of greatest cold. We have fuel and provisions enough. There is nothing to stop us, and we should be culpable, in my opinion, if we allowed ourselves to abandon the project."

"Very well, captain, I'll go along with you."

"That's right; I never doubted you," said Hatteras. "We shall succeed, and England will have all the glory."

"But there is an American among us!" said Johnson.

Hatteras could not repress an impatient exclamation.

"I know it!" he said, in a stern voice.

"We cannot leave him behind," added the Doctor.

"No, we can't," repeated Hatteras, almost mechanically.

"And he will be sure to go too."

"Yes, he will go too; but who will command?"

"You, captain."

"And if you all obey my orders, will the Yankee refuse?"

"I shouldn't think so; but suppose he should, what can be done?"

"He and I must fight it out, then."

The three Englishmen looked at Hatteras, but said nothing. Then the Doctor asked how they were to go.

"By the coast, as far as possible," was the reply.

"But what if we find open water, as is likely enough?"

"Well, we'll go across it."

"But we have no boat."

Hatteras did not answer, and looked embarrassed.

"Perhaps," suggested Bell, "we might make a ship out of some of the planks of the *Porpoise*."

"Never!" exclaimed Hatteras, vehemently.

"Never!" said Johnson.

The Doctor shook his head. He understood the feeling of the captain.

"Never!" reiterated Hatteras. "A boat made out of an American ship would be an American!"

"But, captain——" began Johnson.

The Doctor made a sign to the old boatswain not to press the subject further, and resolved in his own mind to reserve the question for discussion at a more opportune moment. He managed to turn the conversation to other matters, till it abruptly terminated by the entrance of Altamont.

This ended the day, and the night passed quietly without the least disturbance. The bears had evidently disappeared.

CHAPTER XII

IMPRISONED IN DOCTOR'S HOUSE

The first business next day was to arrange for a hunt. It was settled that Altamont, Bell, and Hatteras should form the party, while Clawbonny should go and explore as far as Isle Johnson, and make some hydrographic notes and Johnson should remain behind to keep house.

The three hunters soon completed their preparations. They armed themselves each with a double barrelled revolver and a rifle, and took plenty of powder and shot. Each man also carried in his belt his indispensable snow knife and hatchet, and a small supply of pemmican in case night should surprise them before their return.

Thus equipped, they could go far, and might count on a good supply of game.

At eight o'clock they started, accompanied by Duk, who frisked and gambolled with delight. They went up the hill to the east, across the cone, and down into the plain below.

The Doctor next took his departure, after agreeing with Johnson on a signal of alarm in case of danger.

The old boatswain was left alone, but he had plenty to do. He began by unfastening the Greenland dogs, and letting them out for a run after their long, wearisome confinement. Then he attended to divers housekeeping matters. He had to replenish the stock of combustibles and provisions, to arrange the store-houses, to mend several broken utensils, to repair the rents in coverlets, and get new shoes ready for summer excursions. There was no lack of work, and the old sailor's nimble clever fingers could do anything.

While his hands were busy, his mind was occupied with the conversation of the preceding evening. He thought with regret over the captain's obstinacy, and yet he felt that there was something grand and even heroic in his determination that neither an American nor an American ship should first touch the Pole.

The hunters had been gone about an hour when Johnson suddenly heard the report of a gun.

"Capital!" he exclaimed. "They have found something, and pretty quickly too, for me to hear their guns so distinctly. The atmosphere must be very clear."

A second and a third shot followed.

"Bravo!" again exclaimed the boatswain; "they must have fallen in luck's way!"

But when three more shots came in rapid succession, the old man turned pale, and a horrible thought crossed his mind, which made him rush out and climb hastily to the top of the cone. He shuddered at the sight which met his eyes. The three hunters, followed by Duk, were tearing home at full speed, followed by the five huge bears! Their six balls had evidently taken no effect, and the terrible monsters were close on their heels. Hatteras, who brought up the rear, could only manage to keep off his pursuers by flinging down one article after another—first his cap, then his hatchet, and, finally, his gun. He knew that the inquisitive bears would stop and examine every object, sniffing all round it, and this gave him a little time, otherwise he could not have escaped, for these animals outstrip the fleetest horse, and one monster was so near that Hatteras had to brandish his knife vigorously, to ward off a tremendous blow of his paw.

At last, though panting and out of breath, the three men reached Johnson safely, and slid down the rock with him into the snow-house. The bears stopped short on the upper plateau, and Hatteras and his companions lost no time in barring and barricading them out.

"Here we are at last!" exclaimed Hatteras; "we can defend ourselves better now. It is five against five."

"Four!" said Johnson in a frightened voice.

"How?"

"The Doctor!" replied Johnson, pointing to the empty sitting-room.

"Well, he is in Isle Johnson."

"A bad job for him," said Bell.

"But we can't leave him to his fate, in this fashion," said Altamont.

"No, let's be off to find him at once," replied Hatteras.

He opened the door, but soon shut it, narrowly escaping a bear's hug.

"They are there!" he exclaimed.

"All?" asked Bell.

"The whole pack."

Altamont rushed to the windows, and began to fill up the deep embrasure with blocks of ice, which he broke off the walls of the house.

His companions followed his example silently. Not a sound was heard but the low, deep growl of Duk.

To tell the simple truth, however, it was not their own danger that occupied their thoughts, but their absent friend, the Doctor's. It was for him they trembled, not for themselves. Poor Clawbonny, so good and devoted as he had been to every member of the little colony! This was the first time they had been separated from him. Extreme peril, and most likely a frightful death awaited him, for he might return unsuspectingly to Fort Providence, and find himself in the power of these ferocious animals.

"And yet," said Johnson, "unless I am much mistaken, he must be on guard. Your repeated shots cannot but have warned him. He must surely be aware that something unusual has happened."

"But suppose he was too far away to hear them," replied Altamont, "or has not understood the cause of them? It is ten chances to one but he'll come quickly back, never imagining the danger. The bears are screened from sight by the crag completely."

"We must get rid of them before he comes," said Hatteras.

"But how?" asked Bell.

It was difficult to reply to this, for a sortie was out of the question. They had taken care to barricade the entrance passage, but the bears could easily find a way in if they chose. So it was thought advisable to keep a close watch on their movements outside, by listening attentively in each room, so as to be able to resist all attempts at invasion.

They could hear them distinctly prowling about, growling and scraping the walls with their enormous paws.

However, some action must be taken speedily, for time was passing. Altamont resolved to try a port-hole through which he might fire on his assailants. He had soon scooped out a hole in the wall, but his gun was hardly pushed through, when it was seized with irresistible force, and wrested from his grasp before he could even fire.

"Confound it!" he exclaimed, "we're no match for them."

And he hastened to stop up the breach as fast as possible.

This state of things had lasted upwards of an hour, and there seemed no prospect of a termination. The question of a *sortie* began now to be seriously discussed. There was little chance of success, as the bears could not be attacked separately, but Hatteras and his companions had grown so impatient, and it must be confessed were also so much ashamed of being kept in prison by beasts, that they would even have dared the risk if the captain had not suddenly thought of a new mode of defence.

He took Johnson's furnace-poker, and thrust it into the stove while he made an opening in the snow wall, or rather a partial opening, for he left a thin sheet of ice on the outer side. As soon as the poker was red hot, he said to his comrades who stood eagerly watching him, wondering what he was going to do—

"This red-hot bar will keep off the bears when they try to get hold of it, and we shall be able easily to fire across it without letting them snatch away our guns."

"A good idea," said Bell, posting himself beside Altamont.

Hatteras withdrew the poker, and instantly plunged it in the wall. The melting snow made a loud hissing noise, and two bears ran and made a snatch at the glowing bar; but they fell back with a terrible howl, and at the same moment four shots resounded, one after the other.

"Hit!" exclaimed Altamont.

"Hit!" echoed Bell.

"Let us repeat the dose," said Hatteras, carefully stopping up the opening meantime.

The poker was again thrust into the fire, and in a few minutes was ready for Hatteras to recommence operations.

Altamont and Bell reloaded their guns, and took their places; but this time the poker would not pass through.

"Confound the beasts!" exclaimed the impetuous American.

"What's the matter?" asked Johnson.

"What's the matter? Why, those plaguey animals are piling up block after block, intending to bury us alive!"

"Impossible!"

"Look for yourself; the poker can't get through. I declare it is getting absurd now."

It was worse than absurd, it was alarming. Things grew worse. It was evident that the bears meant to stifle their prey, for the sagacious animals were heaping up huge masses, which would make escape impossible.

"It is too bad," said old Johnson, with a mortified look. "One might put up with men, but bears!"

Two hours elapsed without bringing any relief to the prisoners; to go out was impossible, and the thick walls excluded all sound. Altamont walked impatiently up and down full of exasperation and excitement at finding himself worsted for once. Hatteras could think of nothing but the Doctor, and of the serious peril which threatened him.

"Oh, if Mr. Clawbonny were only here!" said Johnson.

"What could he do?" asked Altamont.

"Oh, he'd manage to get us out somehow."

"How, pray?" said the American, crossly.

"If I knew that I should not need him. However, I know what his advice just now would be."

"What?"

"To take some food; that can't hurt us. What do you say, Mr. Altamont?"

"Oh, let's eat, by all means, if that will please you, though we're in a ridiculous, not to say humiliating, plight."

"I'll bet you we'll find a way out after dinner."

No one replied, but they seated themselves round the table.

Johnson, trained in Clawbonny's school, tried to be brave and unconcerned about the danger, but he could scarcely manage it. His jokes stuck in his throat. Moreover, the whole party began to feel uncomfortable. The atmosphere was getting dense, for every opening was hermetically sealed. The stoves would hardly draw, and it was evident would soon go out altogether for want of oxygen.

Hatteras was the first to see their fresh danger, and he made no attempt to hide it from his companions.

"If that is the case," said Altamont, "we must get out at all risks."

"Yes," replied Hatteras; "but let us wait till night. We will make a hole in the roof, and let in a provision of air, and then one of us can fire out of it on the bears."

"It is the only thing we can do, I suppose," said Altamont.

So it was agreed; but waiting was hard work, and Altamont could not refrain from giving vent to his impatience by thundering maledictions on the bears, and abusing the ill fate which had placed them in such an awkward and humbling predicament. "It was beasts versus men," he said, "and certainly the men cut a pretty figure."

CHAPTER XIII.

THE MINE.

Night drew on, and the lamp in the sitting-room already began to burn dim for want of oxygen.

At eight o'clock the final arrangements were completed, and all that remained to do was to make an opening in the roof.

They had been working away at this for some minutes, and Bell was showing himself quite an adept in the business, when Johnson, who had been keeping watch in the sleeping room, came hurriedly in to his companions, pulling such a long face, that the captain asked immediately what was the matter?

"Nothing exactly," said the old sailor, "and yet—"

"Come, out with it!" exclaimed Altamont.

"Hush! don't you hear a peculiar noise?"

"Where?"

"Here, on this side, on the wall of the room."

Bell stopped working, and listened attentively like the rest. Johnson was right; a noise there certainly was on the side wall, as if some one were cutting the ice.

"Don't you hear it?" repeated Johnson.

"Hear it? Yes, plain enough," replied Altamont.

"Is it the bears?" asked Bell.

"Most assuredly."

"Well; they have changed their tactics," said old Johnson, "and given up the idea of suffocating us."

"Or may be they suppose we are suffocated by now," suggested the American, getting furious at his invisible enemies.

"They are going to attack us," said Bell.

"Well, what of it?" returned Hatteras.

"We shall have a hand-to-hand struggle, that's all."

"And so much the better," added Altamont; "that's far more to my taste; I have had enough of invisible foes—let me see my antagonist, and then I can fight him."

"Ay," said Johnson; "but not with guns. They would be useless here."

"With knife and hatchet then," returned the American.

The noise increased, and it was evident that the point of attack was the angle of the wall formed by its junction with the cliff.

"They are hardly six feet off now," said the boatswain.

"Right, Johnson!" replied Altamont; "but we have time enough to be ready for them."

And seizing a hatchet, he placed himself in fighting attitude, planting his right foot firmly forward and throwing himself back.

Hatteras and the others followed his example, and Johnson took care to load a gun in case of necessity.

Every minute the sound came nearer, till at last only a thin coating separated them from their assailants.

Presently this gave way with a loud crack, and a huge dark mass rolled over into the room.

Altamont had already swung his hatchet to strike, when he was arrested by a well-known voice, exclaiming—

"For Heaven's sake, stop!"

"The Doctor! the Doctor!" cried Johnson.

And the Doctor it actually was who had tumbled in among them in such undignified fashion.

"How do ye do, good friends?" he said, picking himself smartly up.

His companions stood stupefied for a moment, but joy soon loosened their tongues, and each rushed eagerly forward to welcome his old comrade with a loving embrace. Hatteras was for once fairly overcome with emotion, and positively hugged him like a child.

"And is it really you, Mr. Clawbonny?" said Johnson.

"Myself and nobody else, my old fellow. I assure you I have been far more uneasy about you than you could have been about me."

"But how did you know we had been attacked by a troop of bears?" asked Altamont. "What we were most afraid of was that you would come quickly back to Fort Providence, never dreaming of danger."

"Oh, I saw it all. Your repeated shots gave me the alarm. When you commenced firing I was beside the wreck of the *Porpoise*, but I climbed up a hummock, and discovered five bears close on your heels. Oh, how anxious I was for you! But when I saw you disappear down the cliff, while the bears stood hesitating on the edge, as if uncertain what to do, I felt sure that you had managed to get safely inside the house and barricade it. I crept cautiously nearer, sometimes going on all-fours, sometimes slipping between great blocks of ice, till I came at last quite close to our fort, and then I found the bears working away like beavers. They were prowling about the snow, and dragging enormous blocks of ice towards the house, piling them up like a wall, evidently intending to bury you alive. It is a lucky thing they did not take it into their heads to dash down the blocks from the summit of the cone, for you must have been crushed inevitably."

"But what danger you were in, Mr. Clawbonny," said Bell. "Any moment they might have turned round and attacked you."

"They never thought of it even. Johnson's Greenland dogs came in sight several times, but they did not take the trouble to go after them. No, they imagined themselves sure of a more savoury supper!"

"Thanks for the compliment!" said Altamont, laughing.

"Oh, there is nothing to be proud of. When I saw what the bears were up to, I determined to get back to you by some means or other. I waited till night, but as soon as it got dark I glided noiselessly along towards the powder-magazine. I had my reasons for choosing that point from which to work my way hither, and I speedily commenced operations with my snow-knife. A famous tool it is. For three mortal hours I have been hacking and heaving away, but here I am at last tired enough and starving, but still safe here."

"To share our fate!" said Altamont.

"No, to save you all; but, for any sake, give me a biscuit and a bit of meat, for I feel sinking for want of food."

A substantial meal was soon before him, but the vivacious little man could talk all the while he was eating, and was quite ready to answer any questions.

"Did you say *to save us*?" asked Bell.

"Most assuredly!" was the reply.

"Well, certainly, if you found your way in, we can find our way out by the same road."

"A likely story, and leave the field clear for the whole pack to come in and find out our stores. Pretty havoc they would make!"

"No, we must stay here," said Hatteras.

"Of course we must," replied Clawbonny, "but we'll get rid of the bears for all that."

"I told you so," said Johnson, rubbing his hands. "I knew nothing was hopeless if Mr. Clawbonny was here; he has always some expedient in his wise head."

"My poor head is very empty, I fear, but by dint of rummaging perhaps I——"

"Doctor," interrupted Altamont, "I suppose there is no fear of the bears getting in by the passage you have made?"

"No, I took care to stop up the opening thoroughly, and now we can reach the powder-magazine without letting them see us."

"All right; and now will you let us have your plan of getting rid of these comical assailants?"

"My plan is quite simple, and part of the work is done already."

"What do you mean?"

"You shall see. But I am forgetting that I brought a companion with me."

"What do you say?" said Johnson.

"I have a companion to introduce to you," replied the Doctor, going out again into the passage, and bringing back a dead fox, newly killed.

"I shot it this morning," he continued, "and never did fox come more opportunely."

"What on earth do you mean?" asked Altamont.

"I mean to blow up the bears *en masse* with 100 lbs of powder."

"But where is the powder?" exclaimed his friend.

"In the magazine. This passage will lead to it. I made it purposely."

"And where is the mine to be?" inquired Altamont.

"At the furthest point from the house and stores."

"And how will you manage to entice the bears there, all to one spot?"

"I'll undertake that business; but we have talked enough, let us set to work. We have a hundred feet more to add to our passage to-night, and that is no easy matter, but as there are five of us, we can take turns at it. Bell will begin, and we will lie down and sleep meantime."

"Well, really," said Johnson, "the more I think of it, the more feasible seems the Doctor's plan."

"It is a sure one, anyway," said Clawbonny.

"So sure that I can feel the bear's fur already on my shoulder. Well, come, let's begin then."

Away he went into the gloomy passage, followed by Bell, and in a few moments they had reached the powder-magazine, and stood among the well- arranged barrels. The Doctor pointed out to his companion the exact spot where he began excavating, and then left him to his task, at which he laboured diligently for about an hour, when Altamont came to relieve him. All the snow he had dug out was taken to the kitchen and melted, to prevent its taking up room.

The captain succeeded Altamont, and was followed by Johnson. In ten hours—that is to say, about eight in the morning—the gallery was entirely open.

With the first streak of day, the Doctor was up to reconnoitre the position of the enemy. The patient animals were still occupying their old position, prowling up and down and growling. The house had already almost disappeared beneath the piled-up blocks of ice, but even while he gazed a council of war seemed being held, which evidently resulted in the determination to alter the plan of action, for suddenly all the five bears began vigorously to pull down these same heaped-up blocks.

"What are they about?" asked Hatteras, who was standing beside him.

"Well, they look to me to be bent on demolishing their own work, and getting right down to us as fast as possible; but wait a bit, my gentlemen, we'll demolish you first. However, we have not a minute to lose."

Hastening away to the mine, he had the chamber where the powder was to be lodged enlarged the whole breadth and height of the sloping rock against which the wall leaned, till the upper part was about a foot thick, and had to be propped up to prevent its falling in. A strong stake was fixed firmly on the granite foundation, on the top of which the dead fox was fastened. A rope was attached to the lower part of the stake, sufficiently long to reach the powder stores.

"This is the bait," he said, pointing to the dead fox, "and here is the mine," he added, rolling in a keg of powder containing about 100 lbs.

"But, Doctor," said Hatteras, "won't that blow us up too, as well as the bears?"

"No, we shall be too far from the scene of explosion. Besides, our house is solid, and we can soon repair the walls even if they should get a bit shaken."

"And how do you propose to manage?" asked Altamont.

"See! By hauling in this rope we lower the post which props up the roof, and make it give way, and bring up the dead fox to light, and I think you will agree with me that the bears are so famished with their long fasting, that they won't lose much time in rushing towards their unexpected meal. Well, just at that very moment, I shall set fire to the mine, and blow up both the guests and the meal."

"Capital! Capital!" shouted Johnson, who had been listening with intense interest.

Hatteras said nothing, for he had such absolute confidence in his friend that he wanted no further explanation. But Altamont must know the why and wherefore of everything.

"But Doctor," he said, "can you reckon on your match so exactly that you can be quite sure it will fire the mine at the right moment?"

"I don't need to reckon at all; that's a difficulty easily got over."

"Then you have a match a hundred feet long?"

"No."

"You are simply going to lay a train of powder."

"No, that might miss fire."

"Well, there is no way then but for one of us to devote his life to the others, and go and light the powder himself."

"I'm ready," said Johnson, eagerly, "ready and willing."

"Quite useless my brave fellow," replied the Doctor, holding out his hand. "All our lives are precious, and they will be all spared, thank God!"

"Well, I give it up!" said the American. "I'll make no more guesses."

"I should like to know what is the good of learning physics," said the Doctor, smiling, "if they can't help a man at a pinch like this. Haven't we an electric battery, and long enough lines attached to it to serve our purpose? We can fire our mine whenever we please in an instant, and without the slightest danger."

"Hurrah!" exclaimed Johnson.

"Hurrah!" echoed the others, without heeding whether the enemy heard them or not.

The Doctor's idea was immediately carried out, and the connecting lines uncoiled and laid down from the house to the chamber of the mine, one end of each remaining attached to the electric pile, and the other inserted into the keg of powder.

By nine o'clock everything was ready. It was high time, for the bears were furiously engaged in the work of demolition. Johnson was stationed in the powder-magazine, in charge of the cord which held the bait.

"Now," said Clawbonny to his companions, "load your guns, in case our assailants are not killed. Stand beside Johnson, and the moment the explosion is over rush out."

"All right," said Altamont.

"And now we have done all we can to help ourselves. So may Heaven help us!"

Hatteras, Altamont, and Bell repaired to the powder-magazine, while the Doctor remained alone beside the pile.

Soon he heard Johnson's voice in the distance calling out "Ready."

"All right," was the reply.

Johnson pulled his rope vigorously, and then rushed to the loop-hole to see the effect. The thin shell of ice had given way, and the body of the fox lay among the ruins. The bears were somewhat scared at first, but the next minute had eagerly rushed to seize the booty.

"Fire!" called out Johnson, and at once the electric spark was sent along the lines right into the keg of powder. A formidable explosion ensued; the house was shaken as if by an earthquake, and the walls cracked asunder. Hatteras, Altamont, and Bell hurried out with the guns, but they might spare their shot, for four of the bears lay dead, and the fifth, half roasted, though alive, was scampering away in terror as fast as his legs could carry him.

"Hurrah! Three cheers for Clawbonny," they shouted and overwhelmed the Doctor with plaudits and thanks.

CHAPTER XIV.

AN ARCTIC SPRING.

The prisoners were free, and their joy found vent in the noisiest demonstrations. They employed the rest of the day in repairing the house, which had suffered greatly by the explosion. They cleared away the blocks piled up by the animals, and filled up the rents in the walls, working with might and main, enlivened by the many songs of old Johnson.

Next morning there was a singular rise in the temperature, the thermometer going up to 15° above zero.

This comparative heat lasted several days. In sheltered spots the glass rose as high as 31°, and symptoms of a thaw appeared.

The ice began to crack here and there, and jets of salt water were thrown up, like fountains in an English park. A few days later, the rain fell in torrents.

Thick vapour rose from the snow, giving promise of the speedy disappearance of these immense masses. The sun's pale disc became deeper in colour, and remained longer above the horizon. The night was scarcely longer than three hours.

Other tokens of spring's approach were manifest of equal significance, the birds were returning in flocks, and the air resounded with their deafening cries. Hares were seen on the shores of the bay, and mice in such abundance that their burrows completely honeycombed the ground.

The Doctor drew the attention of his companions to the fact, that almost all these animals were beginning to lose their white winter dress, and would soon put on summer attire, while nature was already providing mosses, and poppies, and saxifragas, and short grass for their sustenance. A new world lay beneath that melting snow.

But with these inoffensive animals came back their natural enemies. Foxes and wolves arrived in search of their prey, and dismal howls broke the silence of the short night.

Arctic wolves closely resemble dogs, and their barking would deceive the most practised ears; even the canine race themselves have been deceived by it. Indeed, it seems as if the wily animals employed this ruse to attract the dogs, and make them their prey. Several navigators have mentioned the fact, and the Doctor's own experience confirmed it. Johnson took care not to let his Greenlanders loose; of Duk there was little fear; nothing could take him in.

For about a fortnight hunting was the principal occupation. There was an abundant supply of fresh meat to be had. They shot partridges, ptarmigans, and snow ortolans, which are delicious eating. The hunters never went far from Fort Providence, for game was so plentiful that it seemed waiting their guns, and the whole bay presented an animated appearance.

The thaw, meanwhile, was making rapid progress. The thermometer stood steadily at 32° above zero, and the water ran down the mountain sides in cataracts, and dashed in torrents through the ravines.

The Doctor lost no time in clearing about an acre of ground, in which he sowed the seeds of anti-scorbutic plants. He just had the pleasure of seeing tiny little green leaves begin to sprout, when the cold returned in full force.

In a single night, the thermometer lost nearly 40°; it went down to 8° below zero. Everything was frozen—birds, quadrupeds, amphibia disappeared as if by magic; seal-holes reclosed, and the ice once more became hard as granite.

The change was most striking; it occurred on the 18th of May, during the night. The Doctor was rather disappointed at having all his work to do again, but Hatteras bore the grievance most unphilosophically, as it interfered with all his plans of speedy departure.

"Do you think we shall have a long spell of this weather, Mr. Clawbonny?" asked Johnson.

"No, my friend, I don't; it is a last blow from the cold. You see these are his dominions, and he won't be driven out without making some resistance."

"He can defend himself pretty well," said Bell, rubbing his face.

"Yes; but I ought to have waited, and not have wasted my seed like an ignoramus; and all the more as I could, if necessary, have made them sprout by the kitchen stoves."

"But do you mean to say," asked Altamont, "that you might have anticipated the sudden change?"

"Of course, and without being a wizard. I ought to have put my seed under the protection of Saint Paucratius and the other two saints, whose fête days fall this month."

"Absurd! Pray tell me what they have to do with it? What influence can they possibly have on the temperature?"

"An immense one, if we are to believe horticulturists, who call them the patron saints of the frost."

"And for what reason?"

"Because generally there is a periodical frost in the month of May, and it is coldest from the 11th to the 13th. That is the fact."

"And how is it explained?"

"In two ways. Some say that a larger number of asteroids come between the earth and the sun at this time of year, and others that the mere melting of the snow necessarily absorbs a large amount of heat, and accounts for the low temperature. Both theories are plausible enough, but the fact remains whichever we accept, and I ought to have remembered it."

The Doctor was right, for the cold lasted till the end of the month, and put an end to all their hunting expeditions. The old monotonous life in-doors recommenced, and was unmarked by any incident except a serious illness which suddenly attacked Bell. This was violent quinsy, but, under the Doctor's skilful treatment, it was soon cured. Ice was the only remedy he employed, administered in small pieces, and in twenty-four hours Bell was himself again.

During this compulsory leisure, Clawbonny determined to have a talk with the captain on an important subject—the building of a sloop out of the planks of the *Porpoise*.

The Doctor hardly knew how to begin, as Hatteras had declared so vehemently that he would never consent to use a morsel of American wood; yet it was high time he were brought to reason, as June was at hand, the only season for distant expeditions, and they could not start without a ship.

He thought over it a long while, and at last drew the captain aside, and said in the kindest, gentlest way—

"Hatteras, do you believe I'm your friend?"

"Most certainly I do," replied the captain, earnestly; "my best, indeed my only friend."

"And if I give you a piece of advice without your asking, will you consider my motive is perfectly disinterested?"

"Yes, for I know you have never been actuated by self-interest. But what are you driving at?"

"Wait, Hatteras, I have one thing more to ask. Do you look on me as a true-hearted Englishman like yourself, anxious for his country's glory?"

Hatteras looked surprised, but simply said—

"I do."

"You desire to reach the North Pole," the Doctor went on; "and I understand and share your ambition, but to achieve your object you must employ the right means."

"Well, and have I not sacrificed everything for it?"

"No, Hatteras, you have not sacrificed your personal antipathies. Even at this very moment I know you are in the mood to refuse the indispensable conditions of reaching the pole."

"Ah! it is the boat you want to talk about, and that man——"

"Hatteras, let us discuss the question calmly, and examine the case on all sides. The coast on which we find ourselves at present may terminate abruptly; we have no proof that it stretches right away to the pole; indeed, if your present information prove correct, we ought to come to an open sea during the summer months. Well, supposing we reach this Arctic Ocean and find it free from ice and easy to navigate, what shall we do if we have no ship?"

Hatteras made no reply.

"Tell me, now, would you like to find yourself only a few miles from the pole and not be able to get to it?"

Hatteras still said nothing, but buried his head in his hands.

"Besides," continued the Doctor, "look at the question in its moral aspect. Here is an Englishman who sacrifices his fortune, and even his life, to win fresh glory for his country, but because the boat which bears him across an unknown ocean, or touches the new shore, happens to be made of the planks of an American vessel—a cast-away wreck of no use to anyone—will that lessen the honour of the discovery? If you yourself had found the hull of some wrecked vessel lying deserted on the shore, would you have hesitated to make use of it; and must not a sloop built by four Englishmen and manned by four Englishmen be English from keel to gunwale?"

Hatteras was still silent.

"No," continued Clawbonny; "the real truth is, it is not the sloop you care about: it is the man."

"Yes, Doctor, yes," replied the captain. "It is this American I detest; I hate him with a thorough English hatred. Fate has thrown him in my path."

"To save you!"

"To ruin me. He seems to defy me, and speaks as if he were lord and master. He thinks he has my destiny in his hands, and knows all my projects. Didn't we see the man in his true colours when we were giving names to the different coasts? Has he ever avowed his object in coming so far north? You will never get out of my head that this man is not the leader of some expedition sent out by the American government."

"Well, Hatteras, suppose it is so, does it follow that this expedition is to search for the North Pole? May it not be to find the North-West Passage? But anyway, Altamont is in complete ignorance of our object, for neither Johnson, nor Bell, nor myself, have ever breathed a word to him about it, and I am sure you have not."

"Well, let him always remain so."

"He must be told in the end, for we can't leave him here alone."

"Why not? Can't he stay here in Fort Providence?"

"He would never consent to that, Hatteras; and, moreover, to leave a man in that way, and not know whether we might find him safe when we came back, would be worse than imprudent: it would be inhuman. Altamont will come with us; he must come. But we need not disclose our projects; let us tell him nothing, but simply build a sloop for the ostensible purpose of making a survey of the coast."

Hatteras could not bring himself to consent, but said—

"And suppose the man won't allow his ship to be cut up?"

"In that case, you must take the law in your own hands, and build a vessel in spite of him."

"I wish to goodness he would refuse, then!"

"He must be asked before he can refuse. I'll undertake the asking," said Clawbonny.

He kept his word, for that very same night, at supper, he managed to turn the conversation towards the subject of making excursions during summer for hydrographical purposes.

"You will join us, I suppose, Altamont," he said.

"Of course," replied the American. "We must know how far New America extends."

Hatteras looked fixedly at his rival, but said nothing.

"And for that purpose," continued Altamont, "we had better build a little ship out of the remains of the *Porpoise*. It is the best possible use we can make of her."

"You hear, Bell," said the Doctor, eagerly. "We'll all set to work to-morrow morning."

CHAPTER XV.

THE NORTH-WEST PASSAGE.

Next morning, Altamont Bell and the Doctor repaired to the *Porpoise*. There was no lack of wood, for, shattered as the old "three-master" had been by the icebergs, she could still supply the principal parts of a new ship, and the carpenter began his task immediately.

In the end of May, the temperature again rose, and spring returned for good and all. Rain fell copiously, and before long the melting snow was running down every little slope in falls and cascades.

Hatteras could not contain his delight at these signs of a general thaw among the ice-fields, for an open sea would bring him liberty. At last he might hope to ascertain for himself whether his predecessors were correct in their assertions about a polar basin.

This was a frequent topic of thought and conversation with him, and one evening when he was going over all the old familiar arguments in support of his theory, Altamont took up the subject, and declared his opinion that the polar basin extended west as well as east. But it was impossible for the American and Englishman, to talk long about anything without coming to words, so intensely national were both. Dr. Kane was the first bone of contention on this occasion, for the jealous Englishman was unwilling to grant his rival the glory of being a discoverer, alleging his belief that though the brave adventurer had gone far north, it was by mere chance he had made a discovery.

"Chance!" interrupted Altamont, hotly. "Do you mean to assert that it is not to Kane's energy and science that we owe his great discovery?"

"I mean to say that Dr. Kane's name is not worth mentioning in a country made illustrious by such names as Parry, and Franklin, and Ross, and Belcher, and Penny; in a country where the seas opened the North- West Passage to an Englishman—McClure!"

"McClure!" exclaimed the American. "Well, if ever chance favoured anyone it was that McClure. Do you pretend to deny it?"

"I do," said Hatteras, becoming quite excited. "It was his courage and perseverance in remaining four whole winters among the ice."

"I believe that, don't I?" said Altamont, sneeringly. "He was caught among the bergs and could not get away; but didn't he after all abandon his ship, the *Investigator*, and try to get back home? Besides, putting the man aside, what is the value of his discovery? I maintain that the North-West Passage is still undiscovered, for not a single ship to this day has ever sailed from Behring's Straits to Baffin's Bay!"

The fact was indisputable, but Hatteras started to his feet, and said—

"I will not permit the honour of an English captain to be attacked in my presence any longer!"

"You will not permit!" echoed Altamont, also springing erect. "But these are facts, and it is out of your power to destroy them!"

"Sir!" shouted Hatteras, pale with rage.

"My friends!" interposed the Doctor; "pray be calm. This is a scientific point we are discussing."

But Hatteras was deaf to reason now, and said angrily—

"I'll tell you the facts, sir."

"And I'll tell you," retorted the irate American.

"Gentlemen," said Clawbonny, in a firm tone; "allow me to speak, for I know the facts of the case as well as and perhaps better than you, and I can state them impartially."

"Yes, yes!" cried Bell and Johnson, who had been anxiously watching the strife.

"Well, go on," said Altamont, finding himself in the minority, while Hatteras simply made a sign of acquiescence, and resumed his seat.

The Doctor brought a chart and spread it out on the table, that his auditors might follow his narration intelligibly, and be able to judge the merits of McClure for themselves.

"It was in 1848," he said, "that two vessels, the *Herald* and the *Plover*, were sent out in search of Franklin, but their efforts proving ineffectual, two others were despatched to assist them— the *Investigator*, in command of McClure, and the *Enterprise*, in command of Captain Collison. The *Investigator* arrived first in Behring's Straits, and without waiting for her consort, set out with the declared purpose to find Franklin or the North-West Passage. The gallant young officer hoped to push north as far as Melville Sound, but just at the extremity of the Strait, he was stopped by an insurmountable barrier of ice, and forced to winter there. During the long, dreary months, however, he and his officers undertook a journey over the ice-field, to make sure of its communicating with Melville Sound."

"Yes, but he did not get through," said Altamont.

"Stop a bit," replied Clawbonny; "as soon as a thaw set in, McClure renewed his attempt to bring his ship into Melville Sound, and had succeeded in getting within twenty miles, when contrary winds set in, and dragged her south with irresistible violence. This decided the captain to alter his course. He determined to go in a westerly direction; but after a fearful struggle with icebergs, he stuck fast in the first of the series of straits which end in Baffin's Bay, and was obliged to winter in Mercy Bay. His provisions would only hold out eighteen months longer, but he would not give up. He set out on a sledge, and reached Melville Island, hoping to fall in with some ship or other, but all he found in Winter Harbour was a cairn, which contained a document, stating that Captain Austin's lieutenant, McClintock, had been there the preceding year. McClure replaced this document by another, which stated his intention of returning to England by the North-West Passage he had discovered, by Lancaster Sound and Baffin's Bay, and that in the event of his not being heard of, he might be looked for north or west of Melville Island. Then he went back to Mercy Bay with undaunted courage, to pass a third winter. By the beginning of March his stock of provisions was so reduced in consequence of the utter scarcity of game through the severity of the season, that McClure resolved to send half his men to England, either by Baffin's Bay or by McKenzie River and Hudson's Bay. The other half would manage to work the vessel to Europe. He kept all his best sailors, and selected for departure only those to whom a fourth winter would have been fatal. Everything was arranged for their leaving, and the day fixed, when McClure, who was out walking with Lieutenant Craswell, observed a man running towards them, flinging up his arms and gesticulating frantically, and on getting nearer recognized him as Lieutenant Prim, officer on board the *Herald*, one of the ships he had parted with in Behring's Straits two years before.

Captain Kellett, the Commander, had reached Winter Harbour, and finding McClure's document in the cairn, had dispatched his lieutenant in search of him. McClure accompanied him back, and arranged with the captain to send him his batch of invalids. Lieutenant Craswell took charge of these and conveyed them safely to Winter Harbour. Leaving them there he went across the ice four hundred and seventy miles, and arrived at Isle Beechy, where, a few days afterwards, he took passage with twelve men on board the *Phoenix*, and reached London safely on the 7th of October, 1853, having traversed the whole extent between Behring's Straits and Cape Farewell."

"Well, if arriving on one side and leaving at the other is not going through, I don't know what is!" said Hatteras.

"Yes, but he went four hundred and seventy miles over ice-fields," objected Altamont.

"What of that?"

"Everything; that is the gist of the whole argument. It was not the *Investigator* that went through."

"No," replied Clawbonny, "for, at the close of the fourth winter, McClure was obliged to leave her among the ice."

"Well, in maritime expeditions the vessel has to get through, and not the man; and if ever the Northwest Passage is practicable, it will be for ships and not sledges. If a ship cannot go, a sloop must."

"A sloop!" exclaimed Hatteras, discovering a hidden meaning in the words.

"Altamont," said the Doctor, "your distinction is simply puerile, and in that respect we all consider that you are in the wrong."

"You may easily do that," returned the American. "It is four against one, but that will not prevent me from holding my own opinion."

"Keep it and welcome, but keep it to yourself, if you please, for the future," exclaimed Hatteras.

"And pray what right have you to speak to me like this, sir?" shouted Altamont, in a fury.

"My right as captain," returned Hatteras, equally angry.

"Am I to submit to your orders, then?"

"Most assuredly, and woe to you if——"

The Doctor did not allow him to proceed, for he really feared the two antagonists might come to blows. Bell and Johnson seconded his endeavours to make peace, and, after a few conciliatory words, Altamont turned on his heel, and walked carelessly away, whistling "Yankee Doodle." Hatteras went outside, and paced up and down with rapid strides. In about an hour he came back, and retired to bed without saying another word.

CHAPTER XVI.

ARCTIC ARCADIA

On the 29th of May, for the first time, the sun never set. His glowing disc just touched the boundary line of the horizon, and rose again immediately. The period was now entered when the day lasts twenty- four hours.

Next morning there was a magnificent halo; the monarch of day appeared surrounded by a luminous circle, radiant with all the prismatic colours. This phenomenon never lost its charm, for the Doctor, however frequently it occurred, and he always noted carefully down all particulars respecting it.

Before long the feathered tribes began to return, filling the air with their discordant cries. Flocks of bustards and Canadian geese from Florida or Arkansas came flying north with marvellous rapidity, bringing spring beneath their wings. The Doctor shot several, and among them one or two cranes and a solitary stork.

The snow was now fast melting, and the ice-fields were covered with "slush." All round the bay large pools had formed, between which the soil appeared as if some product of spring.

The Doctor recommenced his sowing, for he had plenty of seed; but he was surprised to find sorrel growing already between the half-dried stones, and even pale sickly heaths, trying to show their delicate pink blossoms.

At last it began to be really hot weather. On the 15th of June, the thermometer stood at 57° above zero. The Doctor scarcely believed his eyes, but it was a positive fact, and it was soon confirmed by the changed appearance of the country.

An excursion was made to Isle Johnson, but it turned out to be a barren little islet of no importance whatever, though it gave the old boatswain infinite pleasure to know that those sea girt rocks bore his name.

There was some danger of both house and stores melting, but happily this high temperature proved exceptional, the thermometer seldom averaging much above freezing point.

By the middle of June, the sloop had made good progress, and already presented a shapely appearance. As Bell and Johnson took the work of construction entirely on themselves, the others went hunting, and succeeded in killing several deer, in spite of its being difficult game to approach. Altamont adopted the Indian practice of crawling on all fours, and adjusting his gun and arms so as to simulate horns and deceive the timid animal, till he could get near enough to take good aim.

Their principal object of pursuit, however, was the musk-ox, which Parry had met with in such numbers in Melville Island; but not a solitary specimen was to be seen anywhere about Victoria Bay, and a distant excursion was, therefore, resolved upon, which would serve the double purpose of hunting and surveying the eastern coast.

The three hunters, accompanied by Duk, set out on Monday, the 17th of June, at six in the morning, each man armed with a double-barrelled gun, a hatchet and snow-knife, and provisions for several days.

It was a fine bright morning, and by ten o'clock they had gone twelve miles; but not a living thing had crossed their path, and the hunt threatened to turn out a mere excursion.

However, they went on in hope, after a good breakfast and half-an-hour's rest.

The ground was getting gradually lower, and presented a peculiar appearance from the snow, which lay here and there in ridges unmelted. At a distance it looked like the sea when a strong wind is lashing up the waves, and cresting them with a white foam.

Before long they reached a sort of glen, at the bottom of which was a winding river. It was almost completely thawed, and already the banks were clothed with a species of vegetation, as if the sun had done his best to fertilise the soil.

"I tell you what," said the Doctor, "a few enterprising colonists might make a fine settlement here. With a little industry and perseverance wonders might be done in this country. Ah! if I am not much mistaken, it has some four-footed inhabitants already. Those frisky little fellows know the best spots to choose."

"Hares! I declare. That's jolly! " said Altamont, loading his gun.

"Stop!" cried the Doctor; "stop, you furious hunter. Let the poor little things alone; they are not thinking of running away. Look, they are actually coming to us, I do believe!"

He was right, for presently three or four young hares, gambolling away among the fresh moss and tiny heaths, came running about their legs so fearlessly and trustfully, that even Altamont was disarmed. They rubbed against the Doctor's knees, and let him stroke them till the kind-hearted man could not help saying to Altamont—

"Why give shot to those who come for caresses? The death of these little beasts could do us no good."

"You say what's true, Clawbonny. Let them live!" replied Hatteras.

"And these ptarmigans too, I suppose, and these long-legged plovers," added Altamont, as a whole covey of birds flew down among the hunters, never suspecting their danger. Duk could not tell what to make of it, and stood stupefied.

It was a strange and touching spectacle to see the pretty creatures; they flew on Clawbonny's shoulders, and lay down at his feet as if inviting friendly caresses, and doing their utmost to welcome the strangers. The whole glen echoed with their joyous cries as they darted to and fro from all parts. The good Doctor seemed some mighty enchanter.

The hunters had continued their course along the banks of the river, when a sudden bend in the valley revealed a herd of deer, eight or ten in number, peacefully browsing on some lichens that lay half-buried in the snow. They were charming creatures, so graceful and gentle, male and female, both adorned with noble antlers, wide-spreading and deeply- notched. Their skin had already lost its winter whiteness, and began to assume the brown tint of summer. Strange to say, they appeared not a whit more afraid than the birds or hares.

The three men were now right in the centre of the herd, but not one made the least movement to run away. This time the worthy Doctor had far more difficulty in restraining Altamont's impatience, for the mere sight of such magnificent animals roused his hunting instincts, and he became quite excited; while Hatteras, on the contrary, seemed really touched to see the splendid creatures rubbing their heads so affectionately and trustfully against the good Clawbonny, the friend of every living thing.

"But, I say," exclaimed Altamont, "didn't we come out expressly to hunt?"

"To hunt the musk-ox, and nothing else," replied Clawbonny. "Besides, we shouldn't know what to do with this game, even if we killed it; we have provisions enough. Let us for once enjoy the sight of men and animals in perfect amity."

"It proves no human beings have been here before," said Hatteras.

"True, and that proves something more, these animals are not of American origin."

"How do you make that out?" said Altamont.

"Why, if they had been born in North America they would have known how to treat that mammiferous biped called man, and would have fled at the first glimpse of us. No, they are from the north, most likely from the untrodden wilds of Asia, so Altamont, you have no right to claim them as fellow-countrymen."

"Oh! a hunter doesn't examine his game so closely as all that. Everything is grist that comes to his mill."

"All right. Calm yourself, my brave Nimrod! For my own part, I would rather never fire another shot than make one of these beautiful creatures afraid of me. See, even Duk fraternizes with them. Believe me, it is well to be kind where we can. Kindness is power."

"Well, well, so be it," said Altamont, not at all understanding such scruples. "But I should like to see what you would do if you had no weapon but kindness among a pack of bears or wolves! You wouldn't make much of it."

"I make no pretensions to charm wild beasts. I don't believe much in Orpheus and his enchantments. Besides, bears and wolves would not come to us like these hares, and partridges, and deer."

"Why not? They have never seen human beings either."

"No but they are savage by nature," said Clawbonny, "and ferocity, like wickedness, engenders suspicion. This is true of men as well as animals."

They spent the whole day in the glen, which the Doctor christened "Arctic Arcadia," and when evening came they lay down to rest in the hollow of a rock, which seemed as if expressly prepared for their accommodation.

CHAPTER XVII.

ALTAMONT'S REVENGE.

Next morning, as the fine weather still continued, the hunters determined to have another search for the musk ox. It was only fair to give Altamont a chance, with the distinct understanding that he should have the right of firing, however fascinating the game they might meet. Besides, the flesh of the musk ox, though a little too highly impregnated with the smell, is savoury food, and the hunters would gladly carry back a few pounds of it to Fort Providence.

During the first part of the day, nothing occurred worth mentioning, but they noticed a considerable change in the aspect of the country, and appearances seemed to indicate that they were approaching a hilly region. This New America was evidently either a continent or an island of considerable extent.

Duk was running far ahead of his party when he stopped suddenly short, and began sniffing the ground as if he had caught scent of game. Next minute he rushed forward again with extreme rapidity, and was speedily out of sight. But loud distinct barking convinced the hunters that the faithful fellow had at last discovered the desired object.

They hurried onwards, and after an hour and a half's quick walking, found him standing in front of two formidable looking animals, and barking furiously. The Doctor recognized them at once as belonging to the musk ox, or *Ovibos* genus, as naturalists call it, by the very wide horns touching each other at their base, by the absence of muzzle, by the narrow square chanfrin resembling that of a sheep, and by the very short tail. Their hair was long and thickly matted, and mixed with fine brown, silky wool.

These singular-looking quadrupeds were not the least afraid of Duk, though extremely surprised; but at the first glimpse of the hunters they took flight, and it was no easy task to go after them, for half an hour's swift running brought them no nearer, and made the whole party so out of breath, that they were forced to come to a halt.

"Confound the beasts!" said Altamont.

"Yes, Altamont, I'll make them over to you," replied Clawbonny; "they are true Americans, and they don't appear to have a very favourable idea of their fellow countrymen."

"That proves our hunting prowess," rejoined Altamont.

Meantime the oxen finding themselves no longer pursued, had stopped short. Further pursuit was evidently useless. If they were to be captured at all they must be surrounded, and the plateau which they first happened to have reached, was very favourable for the purpose. Leaving Duk to worry them, they went down by the neighbouring ravines; and got to the one end of the plateau, where Altamont and the Doctor hid themselves behind projecting rocks, while Hatteras went on to the other end, intending to startle the animals by his sudden appearance, and drive them back towards his companions.

"I suppose you have no objection this time to bestow a few bullets on these gentry?" said Altamont.

"Oh, no, it is 'a fair field now and no favour,'" returned Clawbonny.

The oxen had begun to shake themselves impatiently at Duk, trying to kick him off, when Hatteras started up right in front of them, shouting and chasing them back. This was the signal for Altamont and the Doctor to rush forward and fire, but at the sight of two assailants, the terrified animals wheeled round and attacked Hatteras. He met their onset with a firm, steady foot, and fired straight at their heads. But both his balls were powerless, and only served still further to madden the enraged beasts. They rushed upon the unfortunate man like furies, and threw him on the ground in an instant.

"He is a dead man!" exclaimed the Doctor, in despairing accents.

A tremendous struggle was going on in Altamont's breast at the sight of his prostrate foe, and though his first impulse was to hasten to his help, he stopped short, battling with himself and his prejudices. But his hesitation scarcely lasted half a second, his better self conquered, and exclaiming,

"No, it would be cowardly!" he rushed forward with Clawbonny.

Hatteras full well understood how his rival felt, but would rather have died than have begged his intervention. However, he had hardly time to think about it, before Altamont was at his side.

He could not have held out much longer, for it was impossible to ward off the blows of horns and hoofs of two such powerful antagonists, and in a few minutes more he must have been torn to pieces. But suddenly two shots resounded, and Hatteras felt the balls graze his head.

"Courage!" shouted Altamont, flinging away his discharged weapon, and throwing himself right in front of the raging animals. One of them, shot to the heart, fell dead as he reached the spot, while the other dashed madly on Hatteras, and was about to gore the unfortunate captain with his horns, when Altamont plunged his snow knife far into the beast's wide open jaws with one hand, with the other dealt him such a tremendous blow on the head with his hatchet, that the skull was completely split open.

It was done so quickly that it seemed like a flash of lightning, and all was over. The second ox lay dead, and Clawbonny shouted "Hurrah! hurrah!" Hatteras was saved.

He owed his life to the man he hated the most. What a storm of conflicting passions this must have roused in his soul! But where was the emotion he could not master?

However, his action was prompt, whatever his feeling might be. Without a moment's hesitancy, he went up to his rival, and said in a grave voice—

"Altamont, you have saved my life!"

"You saved mine," replied the American.

There was a moment's silence, and then Altamont added—

"We're quits, Hatteras."

"No, Altamont," said the captain; "when the Doctor dragged you out of your icy tomb, I did not know who you were; but you saved me at the peril of your own life, knowing quite well who I was."

"Why, you are a fellow-creature at any rate, and whatever faults an American may have, he is no coward."

"No, indeed," said the Doctor. "He is a man, every inch as much as yourself, Hatteras."

"And like me, he shall have part in the glory that awaits us."

"The glory of reaching the North Pole?" asked Altamont.

"Yes," replied Hatteras, proudly.

"I guessed right, then," said Altamont.

"And you have actually dared to conceive such a project? Oh! it is grand; I tell you it is sublime even to think of it?"

"But tell me," said Hatteras in a hurried manner; "you were not bound for the Pole then yourself?"

Altamont hesitated.

"Come, speak out, man," urged the Doctor.

"Well, to tell the truth, I was not, and the truth is better than self-love. No, I had no such grand purpose in view. I was trying to clear the North-West Passage, and that was all."

"Altamont," said Hatteras, holding out his hand; "be our companion to glory, come with us and find the North Pole."

The two men clasped hands in a warm, hearty grasp, and the bond of friendship between them was sealed.

When they turned to look for the Doctor they found him in tears.

"Ah! friends," he said, wiping his eyes; "you have made me so happy, it is almost more than I can bear' You have sacrificed this miserable nationality for the sake of the common cause. You have said, 'What does it matter if only the Pole is discovered, whether it is by an Englishman or an American?' Why should we brag of being American or English, when we can boast that we are men?"

The good little man was beside himself with joy He hugged the reconciled enemies to his bosom, and cemented their friendship by his own affection to both.

At last he grew calm after at least a twentieth embrace, and said—

"It is time I went to work now. Since I am no hunter, I must use my talents in another direction"

And he began to cut up the oxen so skilfully, that he seemed like a surgeon making a delicate autopsy.

His two companions looked on smiling. In a few minutes the adroit operator had cut off more than a hundred pounds of flesh. This he divided into three parts. Each man took one, and they retraced their steps to Fort Providence.

At ten o'clock they arrived at Doctor's House, where Johnson and Bell had a good supper prepared for them.

But before sitting down to enjoy it, the Doctor exclaimed in a jubilant tone, and pointing to his two companions—

"My dear old Johnson, I took out an American and an Englishman with me, didn't I?"

"Yes, Mr. Clawbonny."

"Well, I bring back two brothers."

This was joyous news to the sailors, and they shook hands warmly with Altamont; while the Doctor recounted all that had passed, and how the American captain had saved the English captain's life. That night no five happier men could have been found than those that lay sleeping in the little snow house.

CHAPTER XVIII.

FINAL PREPARATIONS

Next day the weather changed, the cold returned. Snow, and rain, and tempest came in quick succession for several days.

Bell had completed the sloop, and done his work well, for the little vessel was admirably adapted for the purpose contemplated, being high at the sides and partly decked so as to be able to stand a heavy sea, and yet light enough to be drawn on the sledge without overburdening the dogs.

At last a change of the greatest importance took place. The ice began to tremble in the centre of the bay, and the highest masses became loosened at their base ready to form icebergs, and drift away before the first gale; but Hatteras would not wait for the ice-fields to break up before he started. Since the journey must be made on land, he did not care whether the sea was open or not; and the day of departure was fixed for the 25th of June—Johnson and Bell undertaking the necessary repairs of the sledge.

On the 20th, finding there was space enough between the broken ice to allow the sloop to get through, it was determined to take her a trial trip to Cape Washington.

The sea was not quite open but it would have been impossible to go across on foot.

This short sail of six hours sufficiently tested the powers of the sloop, and proved her excellent qualities. In coming back they witnessed a curious sight; it was the chase of a seal by a gigantic bear. Mr. Bruin was too busily engaged to notice the vessel, or he would have pursued; he was intently watching beside a seal hole with the patience of a true hunter, or rather angler, for he was certainly fishing just then. He watched in absolute silence, without stirring or giving the least sign of life.

But all of a sudden there was a slight disturbance on the surface of the water in the hole, which announced the coming up of the amphibious animal to breathe. Instantly the bear lay flat on his belly with his two paws stretched round the opening.

Next minute up came the seal, but his head no sooner appeared above the water than the bear's paws closed about him like a vice, and dragged him right out. The poor seal struggled desperately, but could not free himself from the iron grasp of his enemy, who hugged him closer and closer till suffocation was complete. Then he carried him off to his den as if the weight were nothing, leaping lightly from pack to pack till he gained *terra firma* safely.

On the 22nd of June, Hatteras began to load the sledge. They put in 200 lbs. of salt meat, three cases of vegetables and preserved meat, besides lime-juice, and flour, and medicines. They also took 200 lbs. of powder and a stock of fire-arms. Including the sloop and the Halkett- boat, there was about 1500 lbs. weight, a heavy

load for four dogs, and all the more as they would have to drag it every day, instead of only four days successively, like the dogs employed by the Esquimaux, who always keep a relay for their sledges. However, the distance to the Pole was not 150 miles at the outside, and they did not intend to go more than twelve miles a day, as they could do it comfortably in a month. Even if land failed them, they could always fall back on the sloop, and finish the journey without fatigue to men or dogs.

All the party were in excellent health, though they had lost flesh a little; but, by attending to the Doctor's wise counsels, they had weathered the winter without being attacked by any of the maladies incident to the climate.

Now, they were almost at their journey's end, and not one doubted of success, for a common bond of sympathy bound fast the five men, and made them strong to persevere.

On Sunday, the 23rd, all was ready, and it was resolved to devote the entire day to rest.

The dwellers on Fort Providence could not see the last day dawn without some emotion. It cost them a pang to leave the snow-hut which had served them in such good stead, and this hospitable shore where they had passed the winter. Take it altogether, they had spent very happy hours there, and the Doctor made a touching reference to the subject as they sat round the table at the evening meal, and did not forget to thank God for his manifest protection.

They retired early to rest, for they needed to be up betimes. So passed the last night in Fort Providence.

CHAPTER XIX.

MARCH TO THE NORTH

Next day at early dawn, Hatteras gave the signal for departure. The well-fed and well-rested dogs were harnessed to the sledge. They had been having a good time of it all the winter, and might be expected to do good service during the summer.

It was six in the morning when the expedition started. After following the windings of the bay and going past Cape Washington, they struck into the direct route for the north, and by seven o'clock had lost sight of the lighthouse and Fort Providence.

During the first two days they made twenty miles in twelve hours, devoting the remainder of the time to rest and meals. The tent was quite sufficient protection during sleep.

The temperature began to rise. In many places the snow melted entirely away, and great patches of water appeared; here and there complete ponds, which a little stretch of imagination might easily convert into lakes. The travellers were often up to their knees, but they only laughed over it; and, indeed, the Doctor was rather glad of such unexpected baths.

"But for all that," he said, "the water has no business to wet us here. It is an element which has no right to this country, except in a solid or vaporous state. Ice or vapour is all very well, but water— never!"

Hunting was not forgotten during the march, for fresh meat was a necessity. Altamont and Bell kept their guns loaded, and shot ptarmigans, guillemots, geese, and a few young hares; but, by degrees, birds and animals had been changing from trustfulness to fear, and had become so shy and difficult to approach, that very often, but for Duk, the hunters would have wasted their powder.

Hatteras advised them not to go more than a mile away, as there was not a day, nor even an hour, to lose, for three months of fine weather was the utmost they could count upon. Besides, the sledge was often coming to difficult places, when each man was needed to lend a helping hand.

On the third day they came to a lake, several acres in extent, and still entirely frozen over. The sun's rays had little access to it, owing to its situation, and the ice was so strong that it must have dated from some remote winter. It was strong enough to bear both the travellers and their sledge, and was covered with dry snow.

From this point the country became gradually lower, from which the Doctor concluded that it did not extend to the Pole, but that most probably this New America was an island.

Up to this time the expedition had been attended with no fatigue. The travellers had only suffered from the intense glare of the sun on the snow, which threatened them with snow-blindness. At another time of the year they might have avoided this by walking during the night, but at present there was no night at all. Happily the snow was beginning to melt, and the brilliancy would diminish as the process of dissolution advanced.

On the 28th of June the thermometer rose to 45°, and the rain fell in torrents. Hatteras and his companions, however, marched stoically on, and even hailed the downpour with delight, knowing that it would hasten the disappearance of the snow.

As they went along, the Doctor often picked up stones, both round ones and flat pebbles, as if worn away by the tide. He thought from this they must be near the Polar Basin, and yet far as the eye could reach was one interminable plain.

There was not a trace of houses, or huts, or cairns visible. It was evident that the Greenlanders had not pushed their way so far north, and yet the famished tribes would have found their account in coming, for the country abounded in game. Bears were frequently seen, and numerous herds of musk-oxen and deer.

On the 29th, Bell killed a fox and Altamont a musk-ox. These supplies of fresh food were very acceptable, and even the Doctor surveyed, with considerable satisfaction, the haunches of meat they managed to procure from time to time.

"Don't let us stint ourselves," he used to say on these occasions; "food is no unimportant matter in expeditions like ours."

"Especially," said Johnson, "when a meal depends on a lucky shot."

"You're right, Johnson; a man does not think so much about dinner when he knows the soup-pot is simmering by the kitchen-fire."

On the 30th, they came to a district which seemed to have been upturned by some volcanic convulsion, so covered was it with cones and sharp lofty peaks.

A strong breeze from the south-east was blowing, which soon increased to a hurricane, sweeping over the rocks covered with snow and the huge masses, of ice, which took the forms of icebergs and hummocks, though on dry land.

The tempest was followed by damp, warm weather, which caused a regular thaw.

On all sides nothing could be heard but the noise of cracking ice and falling avalanches.

The travellers had to be very careful in avoiding hills, and even in speaking aloud, for the slightest agitation in the air might have caused a catastrophe. Indeed, the suddenness is the peculiar feature in Arctic avalanches, distinguishing them from those of Switzerland and Norway. Often the dislodgment of a block of ice is instantaneous, and not even a cannon-ball or thunderbolt could be more rapid in its descent. The loosening, the fall, and the crash happen almost simultaneously.

Happily, however, no accident befel any of the party, and three days afterwards they came to smooth, level ground again.

But here a new phenomenon met their gaze—a phenomenon which was long a subject of patient inquiry among the learned of both hemispheres. They came to a long chain of low hills which seemed to extend for miles, and were all covered on the eastern side with bright red snow.

It is easy to imagine the surprise and half-terrified exclamations of the little company at the sight of this long red curtain; but the Doctor hastened to reassure them, or rather to instruct them, as to the nature of this peculiar snow. He told them that this same red substance had been found in Switzerland, in the heart of the Alps, and that the colour proceeded solely from the presence of certain corpuscles, about the nature of which for a long time chemists could not agree. They could not decide whether these corpuscles were of animal or vegetable origin, but at last it was settled that they belonged to the family of fungi, being a sort of microscopic champignon of the species *Uredo*.

Turning the snow over with his iron-tipped staff, the Doctor found that the colouring matter measured nine feet deep. He pointed this out to his companions, that they might have some idea of the enormous number of these tiny mushrooms in a layer extending so many miles.

This phenomenon was none the less strange for being explained, for red is a colour seldom seen in nature over any considerable area. The reflection of the sun's rays upon it produced the most peculiar effect, lighting up men, and animals, and rocks with a fiery glow, as if proceeding from some flame within. When the snow melted it looked like blood, as the red particles do not decompose. It seemed to the travellers as if rivulets of blood were running among their feet.

The Doctor filled several bottles with this precious substance to examine at leisure, as he had only had a glimpse of the Crimson Cliffs in Baffin's Bay.

This Field of Blood, as he called it, took three hours to get over, and then the country resumed its usual aspect.

CHAPTER XX.

FOOTPRINTS IN THE SNOW.

On the fourth of July there was such an exceedingly dense fog, that it was very difficult to keep the straight course for the north. No misadventure, however, befel the party during the darkness, except the loss of Bell's snow-shoes. At Bell's suggestion, which fired the Doctor's inventive genius, torches were contrived, made of tow steeped in spirits-of-wine and fastened on the end of a stick, and these served somewhat to help them on, though they made but small progress; for, on the sixth, after the fog had cleared off, the Doctor took their bearings, and found that they had only been marching at the rate of eight miles a day.

Determined to make up for lost time, they rose next morning very early and started off, Bell and Altamont as usual going ahead of the rest and acting as scouts. Johnson and the others kept beside the sledge, and were soon nearly two miles behind the guides; but the weather was so dry and clear that all their movements could be distinctly observed.

"What now? " said Clawbonny, as he saw them make a sudden halt, and stoop down as if examining the ground.

"I was just wondering what they are about, myself," replied old Johnson.

"Perhaps they have come on the tracks of animals," suggested Hatteras.

"No," said Clawbonny, "it can't be that."

"Why not?"

"Because Duk would bark."

"Well, it is quite evident they are examining some sort of marks."

"Let's get on, then," said Hatteras; and, urging forward the dogs, they rejoined their companions in about twenty minutes, and shared their surprise at finding unmistakable fresh footprints of human beings in the snow, as plain as if only made the preceding day.

"They are Esquimaux footprints," said Hatteras.

"Do you think so?" asked Altamont.

"There is no doubt of it."

"But what do you make of this, then?" returned Altamont, pointing to another footmark repeated in several places. "Do you believe for a minute that was made by an Esquimaux?"

It was incontestably the print of a European boot—nails, sole, and heel clearly stamped in the snow. There was no room for doubt, and Hatteras exclaimed in amazement—

"Europeans here!"

"Evidently," said Johnson.

"And yet it is so improbable that we must take a second look before pronouncing an opinion," said Clawbonny.

But the longer he looked, the more apparent became the fact. Hatteras was chagrined beyond measure. A European here, so near the Pole!

The footprints extended for about a quarter of a mile, and then diverged to the west. Should the travellers follow them further?

"No," said Hatteras, "let us go on."

He was interrupted by an exclamation from the Doctor, who had just picked up an object that gave still more convincing proof of European origin. It was part of a pocket spy-glass!

"Well, if we still had any doubts about the footmarks, this settles the case at once, at any rate," said Clawbonny.

"Forward!" exclaimed Hatteras so energetically, that instinctively each one obeyed, and the march was resumed forthwith.

The day wore away, but no further sign of the presence of suspected rivals was discovered, and they prepared to encamp for the night.

The tent was pitched in a ravine for shelter, as the sky was dark and threatening, and a violent north wind was blowing.

"I'm afraid we'll have a bad night," said Johnson.

" A pretty noisy one, I expect," replied the Doctor, "but not cold. We had better take every precaution, and fasten down our tent with good big stones."

"You are right, Mr. Clawbonny. If the hurricane swept away our tent, I don't know where we should find it again."

The tent held fast, but sleep was impossible, for the tempest was let loose and raged with tremendous violence.

"It seems to me," said the Doctor, during a brief lull in the deafening roar," as if I could hear the sound of collisions between icebergs and ice-fields. If we were near the sea, I could really believe there was a general break-up in the ice."

"I can't explain the noises any other way," said Johnson.

"Can we have reached the coast, I wonder?" asked Hatteras.

"It is not impossible," replied Clawbonny. "Listen! Do you hear that crash? That is certainly the sound of icebergs falling. We cannot be very far from the ocean."

"Well, if it turn out to be so, I shall push right on over the ice- fields."

"Oh, they'll be all broken up after such a storm as this. We shall see what to-morrow, brings; but all I can say is, if any poor fellows are wandering about in a night like this, I pity them.

The storm lasted for ten hours, and the weary travellers anxiously watched for the morning. About daybreak its fury seemed to have spent itself, and Hatteras, accompanied by Bell and Altamont, ventured to leave the tent. They climbed a hill about three hundred feet high, which commanded a wide view. But what a metamorphosed region met their gaze! All the ice had completely vanished, the storm had chased away the winter, and stripped the soil everywhere of its snow covering.

But Hatteras scarcely bestowed a glance on surrounding objects; his eager gaze was bent on the northern horizon, which appeared shrouded in black mist.

"That may very likely be caused by the ocean," suggested Clawbonny.

"You are right. The sea must be there," was the reply.

"That tint is what we call the *blink* of open water," said Johnson.

"Come on, then, to the sledge at once, and let us get to this unknown ocean," exclaimed Hatteras.

Their few preparations were soon made, and the march resumed. Three hours afterwards they arrived at the coast, and shouted simultaneously, "The sea! the sea!"

"Ay, and open sea!" added Hatteras.

And so it was. The storm had opened wide the Polar Basin, and the loosened packs were drifting in all directions. The icebergs had weighed anchor, and were sailing out into the open sea.

This new ocean stretched far away out of sight, and not a single island or continent was visible.

On the east and west the coast formed two capes or headlands, which sloped gently down to the sea. In the centre, a projecting rock formed a small natural bay, sheltered on three sides, into which a wide river fell, bearing in its bosom the melted snows of winter.

After a careful survey of the coast, Hatteras determined to launch the sloop that very day, and to unpack the sledge, and get everything on board. The tent was soon put up, and a comfortable repast prepared. This important business despatched, work commenced; and all hands were so expeditious and willing, that by five o'clock nothing more remained to be done. The sloop lay rocking gracefully in the little bay, and all the cargo was on board except the tent, and what was required for the night's encampment.

The sight of the sloop suggested to Clawbonny the propriety of giving Altamont's name to the little bay. His proposition to that effect met with unanimous approval, and the port was forthwith dignified by the title of Altamont Harbour.

According to the Doctor's calculations the travellers were now only 9° distant from the Pole. They had gone over two hundred miles from Victoria Bay to Altamont Harbour, and were in latitude 87° 5′ and longitude 118° 35′.

CHAPTER XXI.

THE OPEN SEA.

Next morning by eight o'clock all the remaining effects were on board, and the preparations for departure completed. But before starting the Doctor thought he would like to take a last look at the country and see if any further traces of the presence of strangers could be discovered, for the mysterious footmarks they had met with were never out of his thoughts. He climbed to the top of a height which commanded a view of the whole southern horizon, and took out his pocket telescope. But what was his astonishment, to find he could see nothing through it, not even neighbouring objects. He rubbed his eyes and looked again, but with no better result. Then he began to examine the telescope, the object glass was gone!

The object glass! This explained the whole mystery, foot-prints and all; and with a shout of surprise he hurried down the hill to impart his discovery to the wondering companions, who came running towards him, startled by his loud exclamation, and full of anxiety at his precipitate descent.

"Well, what is the matter now?" said Johnson.

The Doctor could hardly speak, he was so out of breath. At last he managed to gasp out—

"The tracks, footmarks, strangers."

"What?" said Hatteras, "strangers here?"

"No, no, the object glass; the object glass out of my telescope."

And he held out his spy-glass for them to look at.

"Ah! I see," said Altamont; "it is wanting."

"Yes."

"But then the footmarks?"

"They were ours, friends, just ours," exclaimed the Doctor. "We had lost ourselves in the fog, and been wandering in a circle."

"But the boot-marks," objected Hatteras.

"Bell's. He walked about a whole day after he had lost his snow shoes."

"So I did," said Bell.

The mistake was so evident, that they all laughed heartily, except Hatteras, though no one was more glad than he at the discovery.

A quarter of an hour afterwards the little sloop sailed out of Altamont Harbour, and commenced her voyage of discovery. The wind was favourable, but there was little of it, and the weather was positively warm.

The sloop was none the worse for the sledge journey. She was in first-rate trim, and easily managed. Johnson steered, the Doctor, Bell, and the American leaned back against the cargo, and Hatteras stood at the prow, his fixed, eager gaze bent steadily on that mysterious point towards which he felt drawn with irresistible power, like the magnetic needle to the Pole. He wished to be the first to descry any shore that might come in sight, and he had every right to the honour.

The water of this Polar Sea presented some peculiar features worth mentioning. In colour it was a faint ultramarine blue, and possessed such wonderful transparency that one seemed to gaze down into fathomless depths. These depths were lighted up, no doubt, by some electrical phenomenon, and so many varieties of living creatures were visible that the vessel seemed to be sailing over a vast aquarium.

Innumerable flocks of birds were flying over the surface of this marvellous ocean, darkening the sky like thick heavy storm-clouds. Water-fowl of every description were among them, from the albatross to the penguin, and all of gigantic proportions. Their cries were absolutely deafening, and some of them had such immense, wide-spreading wings, that they covered the sloop completely as they flew over. The Doctor thought himself a good naturalist, but he found his science greatly at fault, for many a species here was wholly unknown to any ornithological society.

The good little man was equally nonplussed when he looked at the water, for he saw the most wonderful medusæ, some so large that they looked like little islands floating about among Brobdignagian sea-weeds. And below the surface, what a spectacle met the eye! Myriads of fish of every species; young manati at play with each other; narwhals with their one strong weapon of defence, like the horn of a unicorn, chasing the timid seals; whales of every tribe, spouting out columns of water and mucilage, and filling the air with a peculiar whizzing noise; dolphins, seals, and walruses; sea-dogs and sea-horses, sea-bears and sea-elephants, quietly browsing on submarine pastures; and the Doctor could gaze at them all as easily and clearly as if they were in glass tanks in the Zoological Gardens.

There was a strange supernatural purity about the atmosphere. It seemed charged to overflowing with oxygen, and had a marvellous power of exhilaration, producing an almost intoxicating effect on the brain.

Towards evening, Hatteras and his companions lost sight of the coast. Night came on, though the sun remained just above the horizon; but it had the same influence on animated nature as in temperate zones. Birds, fish, and all the cetacea disappeared and perfect silence prevailed.

Since the departure from Altamont Harbour, the sloop had made one degree further north. The next day brought no signs of land; there was not even a speck on the horizon. The wind was still favourable, and the sea pretty calm. The birds and fishes returned as numerously as on the preceding day, and the Doctor leaning over the side of the vessel, could see the whales and the dolphins, and all the rest of the monsters of the deep, gradually coming up from the clear depths below. On the surface, far as the eye could reach, nothing was visible except a solitary iceberg here and there, and a few scattered floes.

Indeed, but little ice was met with anywhere. The sloop was ten degrees above the point of greatest cold, and consequently in the same temperature as Baffin's Bay and Disko. It was therefore not astonishing that the sea should be open in these summer months.

This is a fact of great practical value, for if ever the whalers can penetrate north as far as the Polar basin, they may be sure of an immediate cargo, as this part of the ocean seems the general reservoir of whales and seals, and every marine species.

The day wore on, but still nothing appeared on the horizon. Hatteras never left the prow of the ship, but stood, glass in hand, eagerly gazing into the distance with anxious, questioning eyes, and seeking to discover, in the colour of the water, the shape of the waves, and the breath of the wind, indications of approaching land.

CHAPTER XXII.

GETTING NEAR THE POLE.

Hour after hour passed away, and still Hatteras persevered in his weary watch, though his hopes appeared doomed to disappointment.

At length, about six in the evening, a dim, hazy, shapeless sort of mist seemed to rise far away between sea and sky. It was not a cloud, for it was constantly vanishing, and then reappearing next minute.

Hatteras was the first to notice this peculiar phenomenon; but after an hour's scrutiny through his telescope, he could make nothing of it.

All at once, however, some sure indication met his eye, and stretching out his arm to the horizon, he shouted, in a clear ringing voice—-

"Land! land!"

His words produced an electrical effect on his companions, and every man rushed to his side.

"I see it, I see it," said Clawbonny.

"Yes, yes, so do I! " exclaimed Johnson.

"It is a cloud," said Altamont.

"Land! land!" repeated Hatteras, in tones of absolute conviction.

Even while he spoke the appearance vanished, and when it returned again the Doctor fancied he caught a gleam of light about the smoke for an instant.

"It is a volcano!" he exclaimed.

"A volcano?" repeated Altamont.

"Undoubtedly."

"In so high a latitude?"

"Why not? Is not Iceland a volcanic island—indeed, almost made of volcanoes, one might say?"

"Well, has not our famous countryman, James Ross, affirmed the existence of two active volcanoes, the Erebus and the Terror, on the Southern Continent, in longitude 170° and latitude 78°? Why, then, should not volcanoes be found near the North Pole?"

"It is possible, certainly," replied Altamont.

"Ah, now I see it distinctly," exclaimed the Doctor." It is a volcano!"

"Let us make right for it then," said Hatteras.

It was impossible longer to doubt the proximity of the coast. In twenty-four hours, probably, the bold navigators might hope to set foot on its untrodden soil. But strange as it was, now that they were so near the goal of their voyage, no one showed the joy which might have been expected. Each man sat silent, absorbed in his own thoughts, wondering what sort of place this Pole must be. The birds seemed to shun it, for though it was evening, they were all flying towards the south with outspread wings. Was it, then, so inhospitable, that not so much as a sea-gull or a ptarmigan could find a shelter? The fish, too, even the large cetacea, were hastening away through the transparent waters. What could cause this feeling either of repulsion or terror?

At last sleep overcame the tired men, and one after another dropped off, leaving Hatteras to keep watch.

He took the helm, and tried his best not to close his eyes, for he grudged losing precious time; but the slow motion of the vessel rocked him into a state of such irresistible somnolence that, in spite of himself, he was soon, like his companions, locked fast in deep slumber. He began to dream, and imagination brought back all the scenes of his past life. He dreamt of his ship, the *Forward*, and of the traitors that had burnt it. Again he felt all the agonies of disappointment and failure, and forgot his actual situation. Then the scene changed, and he saw himself at the Pole unfurling the Union Jack!

While memory and fancy were thus busied, an enormous cloud of an olive tinge had begun to darken sea and sky. A hurricane was at hand. The first blast of the tempest roused the captain and his companions, and they were on their feet in an instant, ready to meet it. The sea had risen tremendously, and the ship was tossing violently up and down on the billows. Hatteras took the helm again, and kept a firm hold of it, while Johnson and Bell baled out the water which was constantly dashing over the ship.

It was a difficult matter to preserve the right course, for the thick fog made it impossible to see more than a few yards off.

This sudden tempest might well seem to such excited men, a stern prohibition against further approach to the Pole; but it needed but a glance at their resolute faces to know that they would neither yield to winds nor waves, but go right on to the end.

For a whole day the struggle lasted, death threatening them each moment; but about six in the evening, just as the fury of the waves seemed at its highest pitch, there came a sudden calm. The wind was stilled as if miraculously, and the sea became smooth as glass.

Then came a most extraordinary inexplicable phenomenon.

The fog, without dispersing, became strangely luminous, and the sloop sailed along in a zone of electric light. Mast, sail, and rigging appeared pencilled in black against the phosphorescent sky with wondrous distinctness. The men were bathed in light, and their faces shone with a fiery glow.

"The volcano!" exclaimed Hatteras.

"Is it possible?" said Bell.

"No, no!" replied Clawbonny. "We should be suffocated with its flames so near."

"Perhaps it is the reflection," suggested Altamont.

"Not that much even, for then we must be near land, and in that case we should hear the noise of the eruption."

"What is it, then?" asked the captain.

"It is a cosmical phenomenon," replied the Doctor, "seldom met hitherto. If we go on, we shall soon get out of our luminous sphere and be back in the darkness and tempest again."

"Well, let's go on, come what may," said Hatteras.

The Doctor was right. Gradually the fog began to lose its light, and then its transparency, and the howling wind was heard not far off. A few minutes more, and the little vessel was caught in a violent squall, and swept back into the cyclone.

But the hurricane had fortunately turned a point towards the south, and left the vessel free to run before the wind straight towards the Pole. There was imminent danger of her sinking, for she sped along at frenzied speed, and any sudden collision with rock or iceberg must have inevitably dashed her to pieces.

But not a man on board counselled prudence. They were intoxicated with the danger, and no speed could be quick enough to satisfy their longing impatience to reach the unknown.

At last they began evidently to near the coast. Strange symptoms were manifest in the air; the fog suddenly rent like a curtain torn by the wind; and for an instant, like a flash of lightning, an immense column of flame was seen on the horizon.

"The volcano! the volcano!" was the simultaneous exclamation.

But the words had hardly passed their lips before the fantastic vision had vanished. The wind suddenly changed to south-east, and drove the ship back again from the land.

"Confound it!" said Hatteras; "we weren't three miles from the coast."

However, resistance was impossible. All that could be done was to keep tacking; but every few minutes the little sloop would be thrown on her side, though she righted herself again immediately obedient to the helm.

As Hatteras stood with dishevelled hair, grasping the helm as if welded to his hand, he seemed the animating soul of the ship.

All at once, a fearful sight met his gaze.

Scarcely twenty yards in front was a great block of ice coming right towards them, mounting and falling on the stormy billows, ready to overturn at any moment and crush them in its descent.

But this was not the only danger that threatened the bold navigators. The iceberg was packed with white bears, huddling close together, and evidently beside themselves with terror.

The iceberg made frightful lurches, sometimes inclining at such a sharp angle that the animals rolled pell-mell over each other and set up a loud growling, which mingled with the roar of the elements and made a terrible concert.

For a quarter of an hour, which seemed a whole century, the sloop sailed on in this formidable company, sometimes a few yards distant and sometimes near enough to touch. The Greenland dogs trembled for fear, but Duk was quite imperturbable. At last the iceberg lost ground, and got driven by the wind further and further away till it disappeared in the fog, only at intervals betraying its presence by the ominous growls of its equipage.

The storm now burst forth with redoubled fury. The little barque was lifted bodily out of the water, and whirled round and round with the most frightful rapidity. Mast and sail were torn off, and went flying away through the darkness like some large white bird. A whirlpool began to form among the waves, drawing down the ship gradually by its irresistible suction.

Deeper and deeper she sank, whizzing round at such tremendous speed that to the poor fellows on board, the water seemed motionless. All five men stood erect, gazing at each other in speechless terror. But suddenly the ship rose perpendicularly, her prow went above the edge of the vortex, and getting out of the centre of attraction by her own velocity, she escaped at a tangent from the circumference, and was thrown far beyond, swift as a ball from a cannon's mouth.

Altamont, the Doctor, Johnson, and Bell were pitched flat on the planks. When they got up, Hatteras had disappeared!

It was two o'clock in the morning.

CHAPTER XXIII.

THE ENGLISH FLAG

For a few seconds they seemed stupefied, and then a cry of "Hatteras!" broke from every lip.

On all sides, nothing was visible but the tempestuous ocean. Duk barked desperately, and Bell could hardly keep him from leaping into the waves.

"Take the helm, Altamont," said the Doctor, "and let us try our utmost to find our poor captain."

Johnson and Bell seized the oars, and rowed about for more than an hour; but their search was vain— Hatteras was lost!

Lost! and so near the Pole, just as he had caught sight of the goal!

The Doctor called, and shouted, and fired signals, and Duk made piteous lamentations; but there was no response. Clawbonny could bear up no longer; he buried his head in his hands, and fairly wept aloud.

At such a distance from the coast, it was impossible Hatteras could reach it alive, without an oar or even so much as a spar to help him; if ever he touched the haven of his desire, it would be as a swollen, mutilated corpse!

Longer search was useless, and nothing remained but to resume the route north. The tempest was dying out, and about five in the morning on the 11th of July, the wind fell, and the sea gradually became calm. The sky recovered its polar clearness, and less than three miles away the land appeared in all its grandeur.

The new continent was only an island, or rather a volcano, fixed like a lighthouse on the North Pole of the world.

The mountain was in full activity, pouring out a mass of burning stones and glowing rock. At every fresh eruption there was a convulsive heaving within, as if some mighty giant were respiring, and the masses ejected were thrown up high into the air amidst jets of bright flame, streams of lava rolling down the sides in impetuous torrents. In one part, serpents of fire seemed writhing and wriggling amongst smoking rocks, and in another the glowing liquid fell in cascades, in the midst of purple vapour, into a river of fire below, formed of a thousand igneous streams, which emptied itself into the sea, the waters hissing and seething like a boiling cauldron.

Apparently there was only one crater to the volcano, out of which the columns of fire issued, streaked with forked lightning. Electricity seemed to have something to do with this magnificent panorama.

Above the panting flames waved an immense plume-shaped cloud of smoke, red at its base and black at its summit. It rose with incomparable majesty, and unrolled in thick volumes.

The sky was ash-colour to a great height, and it was evident that the darkness that had prevailed while the tempest lasted, which had seemed quite inexplicable to the Doctor, was owing to the columns of cinders overspreading the sun like a thick curtain. He remembered a similar phenomenon which occurred in the Barbadoes, where the whole island was plunged in profound obscurity by the mass of cinders ejected from the crater of Isle St. Vincent.

This enormous ignivomous rock in the middle of the sea was six thousand feet high, just about the altitude of Hecla.

It seemed to rise gradually out of the water as the boat got nearer. There was no trace of vegetation, indeed there was no shore; the rock ran straight down to the sea.

"Can we land?" said the Doctor.

"The wind is carrying us right to it," said Altamont. "But I don't see an inch of land to set our foot upon."

"It seems so at this distance," said Johnson; "but we shall be sure to find some place to run in our boat at, and that is all we want."

"Let us go on, then," said Clawbonny, dejectedly.

He had no heart now for anything. The North Pole was indeed before his eyes, but not the man who had discovered it.

As they got nearer the island, which was not more than eight or ten miles in circumference, the navigators noticed a tiny fiord, just large enough to harbour their boat, and made towards it immediately. They feared their captain's dead body would meet their eyes on the coast, and yet it seemed difficult for a corpse to lie on it, for there was no shore, and the sea broke on steep rocks, which were covered with cinders above watermark.

At last the little sloop glided gently into the narrow opening between two sandbanks just visible above the water, where she would be safe from the violence of the breakers; but before she could be moored, Duk began howling and barking again in the most piteous manner, as if calling on the cruel sea and stony rocks to yield up his lost master. The Doctor tried to calm him by caresses, but in vain. The faithful beast, as if he would represent the captain, sprang on shore with a tremendous bound, sending a cloud of cinders after him.

"Duk! Duk!" called Clawbonny.

But Duk had already disappeared.

After the sloop was made fast, they all got out and went after him. Altamont was just going to climb to the top of a pile of stones, when the Doctor exclaimed, "Listen!"

Duk was barking vehemently some distance off, but his bark seemed full of grief rather than fury.

"Has he come on the track of some animal, do you think? " asked Johnson.

"No, no!" said Clawbonny, shuddering. "His bark is too sorrowful; it is the dog's tear. He has found the body of Hatteras."

They all four rushed forward, in spite of the blinding cinder-dust, and came to the far-end of a fiord, where they discovered the dog barking round a corpse wrapped in the British flag!

"Hatteras! Hatteras!" cried the Doctor, throwing himself on the body of his friend. But next minute he started up with an indescribable cry, and shouted, "Alive! alive!"

"Yes!" said a feeble voice; "yes, alive at the North Pole, on *Queen's Island*."

"Hurrah for England!" shouted all with one accord.

"And for America!" added Clawbonny, holding out one hand to Hatteras and the other to Altamont.

Duk was not behind with his hurrah, which was worth quite as much as the others.

For a few minutes the joy of recovery of their captain filled all their hearts, and the poor fellows could not restrain their tears.

The Doctor found, on examination, that he was not seriously hurt. The wind threw him on the coast where landing was perilous work, but, after being driven back more than once into the sea, the hardy sailor had managed to scramble on to a rock, and gradually to hoist himself above the waves.

Then he must have become insensible, for he remembered nothing more except rolling himself in his flag. He only awoke to consciousness with the loud barking and caresses of his faithful Duk.

After a little, Hatteras was able to stand up supported by the Doctor, and tried to get back to the sloop.

He kept exclaiming, "The Pole! the North Pole!"

"You are happy now?" said his friend.

"Yes, happy! And are not you? Isn't it joy to find yourself here! The ground we tread is round the Pole! The air we breathe is the air that blows round the Pole! The sea we have crossed is the sea which washes the Pole! Oh! the North Pole! the North Pole!"

He had become quite delirious with excitement, and fever burned in his veins. His eyes shone with unnatural brilliancy, and his brain seemed on fire. Perfect rest was what he most needed, for the Doctor found it impossible to quiet him.

A place of encampment must therefore be fixed upon immediately.

Altamont speedily discovered a grotto composed of rocks, which had so fallen as to form a sort of cave. Johnson and Bell carried in provisions, and gave the dogs their liberty.

About eleven o'clock, breakfast, or rather dinner, was ready, consisting of pemmican, salt meat, and smoking-hot tea and coffee.

But Hatteras would do nothing till the exact position of the island was ascertained; so the Doctor and Altamont set to work with their instruments, and found that the exact latitude of the grotto was 89° 59' 15". The longitude was of little importance, for all the meridians blended a few hundred feet higher.

The 90° of lat. was then only about three quarters of a mile off, or just about the summit of the volcano.

When the result was communicated to Hatteras, he desired that a formal document might be drawn up to attest the fact, and two copies made, one of which should be deposited on a cairn on the island.

Clawbonny was the scribe, and indited the following document, a copy of which is now among the archives of the Royal Geographical Society of London:—

"On this 11th day of July, 1861, in North latitude 89° 59' 15" was discovered *Queen's* Island at the North Pole, by Captain Hatteras, Commander of the brig *Forward* of Liverpool, who signs this, as also all his companions.

"Whoever may find this document is requested to forward it to the Admiralty.

"(Signed) JOHN HATTERAS, Commander

of the *Forward*

"DR. CLAWBONNY

"ALTAMONT, Commander of the *Porpoise*

"JOHNSON, Boatswain

"BELL, Carpenter."

"And now, friends, come to table," said the Doctor, merrily.

Coming to table was just squatting on the ground.

"But who," said Clawbonny, "would not give all the tables and dining-rooms in the world to dine at 89″ 59′ and 15″ N. lat.?"

It was an exciting occasion this first meal at the Pole! What neither ancients nor moderns, neither Europeans, nor Americans, nor Asiatics had been able to accomplish was now achieved, and all past sufferings and perils were forgotten in the glow of success.

"But, after all," said Johnson, after toasts to Hatteras and the North Pole had been enthusiastically drunk, "what is there so very special about the North Pole? Will you tell me, Mr. Clawbonny?"

"Just this, my good Johnson. It is the only point of the globe that is motionless; all the other points are revolving with extreme rapidity."

"But I don't see that we are any more motionless here than at Liverpool."

"Because in both cases you are a party concerned, both in the motion and the rest; but the fact is certain."

Clawbonny then went on to describe the diurnal and annual motions of the earth—the one round its own axis, the extremities of which are the poles, which is accomplished in twenty-four hours, and the other round the sun, which takes a whole year.

Bell and Johnson listened half incredulously, and couldn't see why the earth could not have been allowed to keep still, till Altamont informed them that they would then have had neither day nor night, nor spring, summer, autumn, and winter.

"Ay, and worse still," said Clawbonny, "if the motion chanced to be interrupted, we should fall right into the sun in sixty-four and a half days."

"What! take sixty-four and a half days, to fall?" exclaimed Johnson.

"Yes, we are ninety-five millions of miles off. But when I say the Pole is motionless, it is not strictly true; it is only so in comparison with the rest of the globe, for it has a certain movement of its own, and completes a circle in about twenty-six thousand years. This comes from the precession of the equinoxes."

A long and learned talk was started on this subject between Altamont and the Doctor, simplified, however, as much as possible for the benefit of Bell and Johnson.

Hatteras took no part in it, and even when they went on to speculate about the earth's centre, and discussed several of the theories that had been advanced respecting it, he seemed not to hear; it was evident his thoughts were far away.

Among other opinions put forth was one in our own days, which greatly excited Altamont's surprise. It was held that there was an immense opening at the poles which led into the heart of the earth, and that it was out of the opening that the light of the *Aurora Borealis* streamed. This was gravely stated, and Captain Synness, a countryman of our own, actually proposed that Sir Humphrey Davy, Humboldt, and Arago should undertake an expedition through it, but they refused."

"And quite right too," said Altamont.

"So say I; but you see, my friends, what absurdities imagination has conjured up about these regions, and how, sooner or later, the simple reality comes to light."

CHAPTER XXIV.

MOUNT HATTERAS.

After this conversation they all made themselves as comfortable as they could, and lay down to sleep.

All, except Hatteras; and why could this extraordinary man not sleep like the others?

Was not the purpose of his life attained now? Had he not realized his most daring project? Why could he not rest? Indeed, might not one have supposed that, after the strain his nervous system had undergone, he would long for rest?

But no, he grew more and more excited, and it was not the thought of returning that so affected him. Was he bent on going farther still? Had his passion for travel no limits? Was the world too small for him now he had circumnavigated it.

Whatever might be the cause, he could not sleep; yet this first night at the Pole was clear and calm. The isle was absolutely uninhabited—not a bird was to be seen in this burning atmosphere, not an animal on these scoriae-covered rocks, not a fish in these seething waters. Next morning, when Altamont, and the others awoke, Hatteras was gone. Feeling uneasy at his absence, they hurried out of the grotto in search of him.

There he was standing on a rock, gazing fixedly at the top of the mountain. His instruments were in his hand, and he was evidently calculating the exact longitude and latitude.

The Doctor went towards him and spoke, but it was long before he could rouse him from his absorbing contemplations. At last the captain seemed to understand, and Clawbonny said, while he examined him with a keen scrutinizing glance—

"Let us go round the island. Here we are, all ready for our last excursion."

"The last!" repeated Hatteras, as if in a dream. "Yes!, the last truly, but," he added, with more animation, "the most wonderful."

He pressed both hands on his brow as he spoke, as if to calm the inward tumult.

Just then Altamont and the others came up, and their appearance seemed to dispel the hallucinations under which he was labouring.

"My friends," he said, in a voice full of emotion, "thanks for your courage, thanks for your perseverance, thanks for your superhuman efforts, through which we are permitted to set our feet on this soil."

"Captain," said Johnson, "we have only obeyed orders to you alone belongs the honour."

"No, no!" exclaimed Hatteras, with a violent outburst of emotion, "to all of you as much as to me! To Altamont as much as any of us, as much as the Doctor himself! Oh, let my heart break in your hands, it cannot contain its joy and gratitude any longer."

He grasped the hands of his brave companions as he spoke, and paced up and down as if he had lost all self-control.

"We have only done our duty as Englishmen," said Bell.

"And as friends," added Clawbonny.

"Yes, but all did not do it," replied Hatteras "some gave way. However, we must pardon them—pardon both the traitors and those who were led away by them. Poor fellows! I forgive them. You hear me, Doctor?"

"Yes," replied Clawbonny, beginning to be seriously uneasy at his friend's excitement.

"I have no wish, therefore," continued the captain, "that they should lose the little fortune they came so far to seek. No, the original agreement is to remain unaltered, and they shall be rich—if they ever see England again."

It would have been difficult not to have been touched by the pathetic tone of voice in which Hatteras said this.

"But, captain," interrupted Johnson, trying to joke, "one would think you were making your will!"

"Perhaps I am," said Hatteras, gravely.

"And yet you have a long bright career of glory before you!"

"Who knows?" was the reply.

No one answered, and the Doctor did not dare to guess his meaning; but Hatteras soon made them understand it, for presently he said, in a hurried, agitated manner, as if he could scarcely command himself—

"Friends, listen to me. We have done much already, but much yet remains to be done."

His companions heard him with profound astonishment.

"Yes," he resumed, "we are close to the Pole, but we are not on it."

"How do you make that out," said Altamont.

"Yes," replied Hatteras, with vehemence, "I said an Englishman should plant his foot on the Pole of the world! I said it, and an Englishman shall."

"What!" cried Clawbonny.

"We are still 45" from the unknown point," resumed Hatteras, with increasing animation, "and to that point I shall go."

"But it is on the summit of the volcano," said the Doctor.

"I shall go."

"It is an inaccessible cone!"

"I shall go."

"But it is a yawning fiery crater!"

"I shall go."

The tone of absolute determination in which Hatteras pronounced these words it is impossible to describe.

His friends were stupefied, and gazed in terror at the blazing mountain.

At last the Doctor recovered himself, and began to urge and entreat Hatteras to renounce his project. He tried every means his heart dictated, from humble supplications to friendly threats; but he could gain nothing—a sort of frenzy had come over the captain, an absolute monomania about the Pole.

Nothing but violent measures would keep him back from destruction, but the Doctor was unwilling to employ these unless driven to extremity.

He trusted, moreover, that physical impossibilities, insuperable obstacles would bar his further progress, and meantime finding all protestations were useless, he simply said—

"Very well, since you are bent on it, we'll go too."

"Yes," replied Hatteras, "half-way up the mountain, but not a step beyond. You know you have to carry back to England the duplicate of the document in the cairn——"

"Yes; but——"

"It is settled," said Hatteras, in an imperious tone; "and since the prayers of a friend will not suffice, the captain commands."

The Doctor did not insist longer, and a few minutes after the little band set out, accompanied by Duk.

It was about eight o'clock when they commenced their difficult ascent; the sky was splendid, and the thermometer stood at 52°.

Hatteras and his dog went first, closely followed by the others.

"I am afraid," said Johnson to the Doctor.

"No, no, there's nothing to be afraid of; we are here."

This singular little island appeared to be of recent formation, and was evidently the product of successive volcanic eruptions. The rocks were all lying loose on the top of each other, and it was a marvel how they preserved their equilibrium. Strictly speaking, the mountain was only a heap of stones thrown down from a height, and the mass of rocks which composed the island had evidently come out of the bowels of the earth.

The earth, indeed, may be compared to a vast cauldron of spherical form, in which, under the influence of a central fire, immense quantities of vapours are generated, which would explode the globe but for the safety-valves outside.

These safety-valves are volcanoes, when one closes another opens; and at the Poles where the crust of the earth is thinner, owing to its being flattened, it is not surprising that a volcano should be suddenly formed by the upheaving of some part of the ocean-bed.

The Doctor, while following Hatteras, was closely following all the peculiarities of the island, and he was further confirmed in his opinion as to its recent formation by the absence of water. Had it existed for centuries, the thermal springs would have flowed from its bosom.

As they got higher, the ascent became more and more difficult, for the flanks of the mountain were almost perpendicular, and it required the utmost care to keep them from falling. Clouds of scoriæ and ashes would whirl round them repeatedly, threatening them with asphyxia, or torrents of lava would bar their passage. In parts where these torrents ran horizontally, the outside had become hardened; while underneath was the boiling lava, and every step the travellers took had first to be tested with the iron-tipped staff to avoid being suddenly plunged into the scalding liquid.

At intervals large fragments of red-hot rock were thrown up from the crater, and burst in the air like bomb-shells, scattering the debris to enormous distances in all directions.

Hatteras, however, climbed up the steepest ascents with surprising agility, disdaining the help of his staff.

He arrived before long at a circular rock, a sort of plateau about ten feet wide. A river of boiling lava surrounded it, except in one part, where it forked away to a higher rock, leaving a narrow passage, through which Hatteras fearlessly passed.

Here he stopped, and his companions managed to rejoin him. He seemed to be measuring with his eye the distance he had yet to get over. Horizontally, he was not more than two hundred yards from the top of the crater, but vertically he had nearly three times that distance to traverse.

The ascent had occupied three hours already. Hatteras showed no signs of fatigue, while the others were almost spent.

The summit of the volcano appeared inaccessible, and the Doctor determined at any price to prevent Hatteras from attempting to proceed. He tried gentle means first, but the captain's excitement was fast becoming delirium. During their ascent, symptoms of insanity had become more and more marked, and no one could be surprised who knew anything of his previous history.

"Hatteras," said the Doctor, "it is enough! we cannot go further!"

"Stop, then," he replied, in a strangely altered voice; "I am going higher."

"No, it is useless; you are at the Pole already."

"No, no! higher, higher!"

"My friend, do you know who is speaking to you? It is I, Doctor Clawbonny."

"Higher, higher!" repeated the madman.

"Very well, we shall not allow it—that is all."

He had hardly uttered the words before Hatteras, by a superhuman effort, sprang over the boiling lava, and was beyond the reach of his companions.

A cry of horror burst from every lip, for they thought the poor captain must have perished in that fiery gulf; but there he was safe on the other side, accompanied by his faithful Duk, who would not leave him.

He speedily disappeared behind a curtain of smoke, and they heard his voice growing fainter in the distance, shouting—

"To the north! to the north! to the top of Mount Hatteras! Remember Mount Hatteras!"

All pursuit of him was out of the question; it was impossible to leap across the fiery torrent, and equally impossible to get round it. Altamont, indeed, was mad enough to make an attempt, and would certainly have lost his life if the others had not held him back by main force.

"Hatteras! Hatteras!" shouted the Doctor, but no response was heard save the faint bark of Duk.

At intervals, however, a glimpse of him could be caught through the clouds of smoke and showers of ashes. Sometimes his head, sometimes his arm appeared; then he was out of sight again, and a few minutes later was seen higher up clinging to the rocks. His size constantly decreased with the fantastic rapidity of objects rising upwards in the air. In half-an-hour he was only half his size.

The air was full of the deep rumbling noise of the volcano, and the mountain shook and trembled. From time to time a loud fail was heard behind, and the travellers would see some enormous rock rebounding from the heights to engulph itself in the polar basin below.

Hatteras did not even turn once to look back, but marched straight on, carrying his country's flag attached to his staff. His terrified friends watched every movement, and saw him gradually decrease to microscopic dimensions, while Duk looked no larger than a big rat.

Then came a moment of intense anxiety, for the wind beat down on them an immense sheet of flame, and they could see nothing but the red glare. A cry of agony escaped the Doctor; but an instant afterwards Hatteras reappeared, waving his flag.

For a whole hour this fearful spectacle went on—an hour of battle with unsteady loose rocks and quagmires of ashes, where the foolhardy climber sank up to his waist. Sometimes they saw him hoist himself up by leaning knees and loins against the rocks in narrow, intricate winding paths, and sometimes he would be hanging on by both hands to some sharp crag, swinging to and fro like a withered tuft.

At last he reached the summit of the mountain, the mouth of the crater. Here the Doctor hoped the infatuated man would stop, at any rate, and would, perhaps, recover his senses, and expose himself to no more danger than the descent involved.

Once more he shouted—

"Hatteras! Hatteras!"

There was such a pathos of entreaty in his tone that Altamont felt moved to his inmost soul.

"I'll save him yet!" he exclaimed; and before Clawbonny could hinder him, he had cleared with a bound the torrent of fire, and was out of sight among the rocks.

Meantime, Hatteras had mounted a rock which overhung the crater, and stood waving his flag amidst showers of stones which rained down on him. Duk was by his side; but the poor beast was growing dizzy in such close proximity to the abyss.

Hatteras balanced his staff in one hand, and with the other sought to find the precise mathematical point where all the meridians of the globe meet, the point on which it was his sublime purpose to plant his foot.

All at once the rock gave way, and he disappeared. A cry of horror broke from his companions, and rang to the top of the mountain. Clawbonny thought his friend had perished, and lay buried for ever in the depths of the volcano. A second—only a second, though it seemed an age—elapsed, and there was Altamont and the dog holding the ill-fated Hatteras! Man and dog had caught him at the very moment when he disappeared in the abyss.

Hatteras was saved! Saved in spite of himself; and half-an-hour later be lay unconscious in the arms of his despairing companions.

When he came to himself, the Doctor looked at him in speechless anguish, for there was no glance of recognition in his eye. It was the eye of a blind man, who gazes without seeing.

"Good heavens!" exclaimed Johnson; "he is blind!"

"No," replied Clawbonny, "no! My poor friends, we have only saved the body of Hatteras; his soul is left behind on the top of the volcano. His reason is gone!"

"Insane!" exclaimed Johnson and Altamont, in consternation.

"Insane!" replied the Doctor, and the big tears ran down his cheeks.

CHAPTER XXV.

RETURN SOUTH.

Three hours after this sad *dénouement* of the adventures of Captain Hatteras, the whole party were back once more in the grotto.

Clawbonny was asked his opinion as to what was best to be done.

"Well, friends," he said, "we cannot stay longer in this island; the sea is open, and we have enough provisions. We ought to start at once, and get back without the least delay to Fort Providence, where we must winter."

"That is my opinion, too," said Altamont. "The wind is favourable, so to-morrow we will get to sea."

The day passed in profound dejection. The insanity of the captain was a bad omen and when they began to talk over the return voyage, their hearts failed them for fear. They missed the intrepid spirit of their leader.

However, like brave men, they prepared to battle anew with the elements and with themselves, if ever they felt inclined to give way.

Next morning they made all ready to sail, and brought the tent and all its belongings on board.

But before leaving these rocks, never to return, the Doctor carrying out the intentions of Hatteras, had a cairn erected on the very spot where the poor fellow had jumped ashore. It was made of great blocks placed one on the top of the other, so as to be a landmark perfectly visible while the eruptions of the volcano left it undisturbed. On one of the side stones, Bell chiselled the simple inscription—

JOHN HATTERAS.

The duplicate of the document attesting the discovery of the North Pole was enclosed in a tinned iron cylinder, and deposited in the cairn, to remain as a silent witness among those desert rocks.

This done, the four men and the captain, a poor body without a soul, set out on the return voyage, accompanied by the faithful Duk, who had become sad and downcast.

A new sail was manufactured out of the tent, and about ten o'clock, the little sloop sailed out before the wind.

She made a quick passage, finding abundance of open water. It was certainly easier to get away from the Pole than to get to it.

But Hatteras knew nothing that was passing around him. He lay full length in the boat, perfectly silent, with lifeless eye and folded arms, and Duk lying at his feet. Clawbonny frequently addressed him, but could elicit no reply.

On the 15th they sighted Altamont Harbour, but as the sea was open all along the coast, they determined to go round to Victoria Bay by water, instead of crossing New America in the sledge.

The voyage was easy and rapid. In a week they accomplished what had taken a fortnight in the sledge, and on the 23rd they cast anchor in Victoria Bay.

As soon as the sloop was made fast, they all hastened to Fort Providence. But what a scene of devastation met their eyes! Doctor's House, stores, powder-magazine, fortifications, all had melted away, and the provisions had been ransacked by devouring animals.

The navigators had almost come to the end of their supplies, and had been reckoning on replenishing their stores at Fort Providence. The impossibility of wintering there now was evident, and they decided to get to Baffin's Bay by the shortest route.

"We have no alternative," said Clawbonny; "Baffin's Bay is not more than six hundred miles distant. We can sail as long as there is water enough under our sloop, and get to Jones' Sound, and then on to the Danish settlements."

"Yes," said Altamont; "let us collect what food remains, and be off at once."

After a thorough search, a few cases of pemmican were found scattered here and there, and two barrels of preserved meat, altogether enough for six weeks, and a good supply of powder. It was soon collected and brought on board, and the remainder of the day was employed in caulking the sloop and putting her in good trim.

Next morning they put out once more to sea. The voyage presented no great difficulties, the drift-ice being easily avoided; but still the Doctor thought it advisable, in case of possible delays, to limit the rations to one-half. This was no great hardship, as there was not much work for anyone to do, and all were in perfect health.

Besides, they found a little shooting, and brought down ducks, and geese, and guillemots, or sea turtledoves. Water they were able to supply themselves with in abundance, from the fresh-water icebergs they constantly fell in with as they kept near the coast, not daring to venture out to the open sea in so frail a barque.

At that time of the year, the thermometer was already constantly below freezing point. The frequent rains changed to snow, and the weather became gloomy. Each day the sun dipped lower below the horizon, and on the 30th, for a few minutes, he was out of sight altogether.

However, the little sloop sailed steadily on without stopping an instant. They knew what fatigues and obstacles a land journey involved, if they should be forced to adopt it, and no time was to be lost, for soon the open water would harden to firm ground; already the young ice had begun to form. In these high latitudes there is neither spring nor autumn; winter follows close on the heels of summer.

On the 31st the first stars glimmered overhead, and from that time forwards there was continual fog, which considerably impeded navigation.

The Doctor became very uneasy at these multiplied indications of approaching winter. He knew the difficulties Sir John Ross had to contend with after he left his ship to try and reach Baffin's Bay, and how, after all, he was compelled to return and pass a fourth winter on board. It was bad enough with shelter and food and fuel, but if any such calamity befell the survivors of the *Forward*, if they were obliged to stop or return, they were lost.

The Doctor said nothing of his anxieties to his companions, but only urged them to get as far east as possible.

At last, after thirty days' tolerably quick sailing, and after battling for forty-eight hours against the increasing drift ice, and risking the frail sloop a hundred times, the navigators saw themselves blocked in on all sides. Further progress was impossible, for the sea was frozen in every direction, and the thermometer was only 15° above zero.

Altamont made a reckoning with scrupulous precision, and found they were in 77°15' latitude, and 85° 2' longitude.

"This is our exact position then," said the Doctor. "We are in South Lincoln, just at Cape Eden, and are entering Jones' Sound. With a little more good luck, we should have found open water right to Baffin's Bay. But we must not grumble. If my poor Hatteras had found as navigable a sea at first, he would have soon reached the Pole. His men would not have deserted him, and his brain would not have given way under the pressure of terrible trial."

"I suppose, then," said Altamont, "our only course is to leave the sloop, and get by sledge to the east coast of Lincoln."

"Yes; but I think we should go through Jones' Sound, and get to South Devon instead of crossing Lincoln."

"Why?"

"Because the nearer we get to Lancaster Sound, the more chance we have of meeting whalers."

"You are right; but I question whether the ice is firm enough to make it practicable."

"We'll try," replied Clawbonny.

The little vessel was unloaded, and the sledge put together again. All the parts were in good condition, so the next day the dogs were harnessed, and they started off along the coast to reach the ice-field; but Altamont's opinion proved right. They could not get through Jones' Sound, and were obliged to follow the coast to Lincoln.

At last, on the 24th, they set foot on North Devon.

"Now," said Clawbonny, "we have only to cross this, and get to Cape Warender at the entrance to Lancaster Sound."

But the weather became frightful, and very cold. The snow-storms and tempests returned with winter violence, and the travellers felt too weak to contend with them. Their stock of provisions was almost exhausted, and rations had to be reduced now to a third, that the dogs might have food enough to keep them in working condition.

The nature of the ground added greatly to the fatigue. North Devon is extremely wild and rugged, and the path across the Trauter mountains is through difficult gorges. The whole party—men, and dogs, and sledge alike—were frequently forced to stop, for they could not struggle on against the fury of the elements. More than once despair crept over the brave little band, hardy as they were, and used to Polar sufferings. Though scarcely aware of it themselves, they were completely worn out, physically and mentally.

It was not till the 30th of August that they emerged from these wild mountains into a plain, which seemed to have been upturned and convulsed by volcanic action at some distant period.

Here it was absolutely necessary to take a few days' rest, for the travellers could not drag one foot after the other, and two of the dogs had died from exhaustion. None of the party felt equal to put up the tent, so they took shelter behind an iceberg.

Provisions were now so reduced, that, notwithstanding their scanty rations, there was only enough left for one week. Starvation stared the poor fellows in the face.

Altamont, who had displayed great unselfishness and devotion to the others, roused his sinking energies, and determined to go out and find food for his comrades.

He took his gun, called Duk, and went off almost unnoticed by the rest.

He had been absent about an hour, and only once during that time had they heard the report of his gun; and now he was coming back empty-handed, but running as if terrified.

"What is the matter?" asked the Doctor.

"Down there, under the snow!" said Altamont, speaking as if scared, and pointing in a particular direction.

"What?"

"A whole party of men!"

"Alive?"

"Dead—frozen—and even—"

He did not finish the sentence, but a look of unspeakable horror came over his face.

The Doctor and the others were so roused by this incident, that they managed to get up and drag themselves after Altamont towards the place he indicated.

They soon arrived, at a narrow part at the bottom of a ravine, and what a spectacle met their gaze! Dead bodies, already stiff, lay half- buried in a winding-sheet of snow. A leg visible here, an arm there, and yonder shrunken hands and rigid faces, stamped with the expression of rage and despair.

The Doctor stooped down to look at them more closely, but instantly started back pale and agitated, while Duk barked ominously.

"Horrible, horrible!" he said.

"What is it?" asked Johnson.

"Don't you recognize them?"

"What do you mean?"

"Look and see!"

It was evident this ravine had been but recently the scene of a fearful straggle with cold, and despair, and starvation, for by certain horrible remains it was manifest that the poor wretches had been feeding on human flesh, perhaps while still warm and palpitating; and among them the Doctor recognized Shandon, Pen, and the ill-fated crew of the *Forward!* Their strength had failed; provisions had come to an end; their boat had been broken, perhaps by an avalanche or engulphed in some abyss, and they could not take advantage of the open sea; or perhaps they had lost their way in wandering over these unknown continents. Moreover, men who set out under the excitement of a revolt were not likely to remain long united. The leader of a rebellion has but a doubtful power, and no doubt Shandon's authority had been soon cast off.

Be that as it might, it was evident the crew had come through agonies of suffering and despair before this last terrible catastrophe, but the secret of their miseries is buried with them beneath the polar snows.

"Come away! come away!" said the Doctor, dragging his companions from the scene. Horror gave them momentary strength, and they resumed their march without stopping a minute longer.

CHAPTER XXVI.

CONCLUSION.

It would be useless to enumerate all the misfortunes which befell the survivors of the expedition. Even the men themselves were never able to give any detailed narrative of the events which occurred during the week subsequent to the horrible discovery related in the last chapter. However, on the 9th of September, by superhuman exertions, they arrived at last at Cape Horsburg, the extreme point of North Devon.

They were absolutely starving. For forty-eight hours they had tasted nothing, and their last meal had been off the flesh of their last Esquimaux dog. Bell could go no further, and Johnson felt himself dying.

They were on the shore of Baffin's Bay, now half-frozen over; that is to say, on the road to Europe, and three miles off the waves were dashing noiselessly on the sharp edges of the ice-field.

Here they must wait their chance of a whaler appearing; and for how long?

But Heaven pitied the poor fellows, for the very next day Altamont distinctly perceived a sail on the horizon. Every one knows the torturing suspense that follows such an appearance, and the agonizing dread lest it should prove a false hope. The vessel seems alternately to approach and recede, and too often just at the very moment when the poor castaways think they are saved, the sail begins to disappear, and is soon out of sight.

The Doctor and his companions went through all these experiences. They had succeeded in reaching the western boundary of the ice-field by carrying and pushing each other along, and they watched the ship gradually fade away from view without observing them, in spite of their loud cries for help.

Just then a happy inspiration came to the Doctor. His fertile genius, which had served him many a time in such good stead, supplied him with one last idea!

A floe driven by the current struck against the icefield, and Clawbonny exclaimed, pointing to it—

"This floe!"

His companions could not understand what he meant.

"Let us embark on it! let us embark on it!"

"Oh! Mr. Clawbonny, Mr. Clawbonny," said Johnson, pressing his hand.

Bell, assisted by Altamont, hurried to the sledge, and brought back one of the poles, which he stuck fast on the ice like a mast, and fastened it with ropes. The tent was torn up to furnish a sail, and as soon as the frail raft was ready the poor fellows jumped upon it, and sailed out to the open sea.

Two hours later, after unheard-of exertions, the survivors of the *Forward* were picked up by the *Hans Christian*, a Danish whaler, on her way to Davis' Straits. They were more like spectres than human beings, and the sight of their sufferings was enough. It told its own tale; but the captain received them with such hearty sympathy, and lavished on them such care and kindness, that he succeeded in keeping them alive.

Ten days afterwards, Clawbonny, Johnson, Bell, Altamont, and Captain Hatteras landed at Korsam, in Zealand, an island belonging to Denmark. They took the steamer to Kiel, and from there proceeded by Altona and Hamburg to London, where they arrived on the 13th of the same month, scarcely recovered after their long sufferings.

The first care of Clawbonny was to request the Royal Geographical Society to receive a communication from him. He was accordingly admitted to the next

séance, and one can imagine the astonishment of the learned assembly and the enthusiastic applause produced by the reading of Hatteras' document.

The English have a passion for geographical discovery, from the lord to the cockney, from the merchant down to the dock labourer, and the news of this grand discovery speedily flashed along the telegraph wires, throughout the length and breadth of the kingdom. Hatteras was lauded as a martyr by all the newspapers, and every Englishman felt proud of him.

The Doctor and his companions had the honour of being presented to the Queen by the Lord Chancellor, and they were feted and "lionized" in all quarters.

The Government confirmed the names of "Queen's Island," "Mount Hatteras," and "Altamont Harbour."

Altamont would not part from his companions in misery and glory, but followed them to Liverpool, where they were joyously welcomed back, after being so long supposed dead and buried beneath the eternal snows.

But Dr. Clawbonny would never allow that any honour was due to himself. He claimed all the merit of the discovery for his unfortunate captain, and in the narrative of his voyage, published the next year under the auspices of the Royal Geographical Society, he places John Hatteras on a level with the most illustrious navigators, and makes him the compeer of all the brave, daring men who have sacrificed themselves for the progress of science.

The insanity of this poor victim of a sublime passion was of a mild type, and he lived quietly at Sten Cottage, a private asylum near Liverpool, where the Doctor himself had placed him. He never spoke, and understood nothing that was said to him; reason and speech had fled together. The only tie that connected him with the outside world was his friendship for Duk, who was allowed to remain with him.

For a considerable time the captain had been in the habit of walking in the garden for hours, accompanied by his faithful dog, who watched him with sad, wistful eyes, but his promenade was always in one direction in a particular part of the garden. When he got to the end of this path, he would stop and begin to walk backwards. If anyone stopped him he would point with his finger towards a certain part of the sky, but let anyone attempt to turn him round, and he became angry, while Duk, as if sharing his master's sentiments, would bark furiously.

The Doctor, who often visited his afflicted friend, noticed this strange proceeding one day, and soon understood the reason of it. He saw how it was that he paced so constantly in a given direction, as if under the influence of some magnetic force.

This was the secret: John Hatteras invariably walked towards the North.

The End.

Milton Keynes UK
Ingram Content Group UK Ltd.
UKHW020838260624
444769UK00011B/357

9 781836 572794